SKINNY

Also by Robert Burch

A FUNNY PLACE TO LIVE

TYLER, WILKIN, AND SKEE

YOUNG AMERICA BOOK CLUB

PRESENTS

Skinny

by Robert Burch

ILLUSTRATED BY

DON SIBLEY

The Viking Press · NEW YORK

PRINTED IN THE UNITED STATES OF AMERICA
BY AMERICAN BOOK—STRATFORD PRESS, INC., N.Y.

for the Harwoods:
Mary, John, Bill, and Ann

Contents

1. The Hotel   9
2. The Watermelon-cutting   20
3. R. F. D.   31
4. The Carnival and Calvin   43
5. The Trucks Roll into Town   56
6. Plans   69
7. The Freight Platform at Midnight   80
8. Calvin's Visit   91
9. "This Hotel Ain't Meant to Be Lively"   103
10. Forty Miles Is a Far Piece   113

1 ′′′′′′′′′ *The Hotel*

"You mean you're eleven years old and don't know how to read?" asked the man, propping one foot against the banister.

Skinny continued sweeping the hotel porch. "I'm going on twelve," he said.

"But why can't you read?"

"I just ain't never took it up," said Skinny, thinking it was an aggravation the way some folks promoted book-learning. All he had done was ask the man, one of the highway engineers staying at the hotel, if he would mind reading the weather forecast out loud.

"Have a look for yourself," the man had said, offering him the newspaper.

Any other time Skinny would have taken it and pretended to read. But he was so anxious to know about the weather for tonight that he had admitted his one little failing. And the man carried on as if it were a serious matter. "Don't you go to school?" he was asking now.

"Sure," said Skinny, pushing straggly hair away from his forehead, "two or three weeks every year. But that's not long enough to get the hang of reading."

The man wanted to know why he had never stayed longer. Skinny explained. "Cotton was always ready to be picked not long after school got under way, and Pa would keep me home to help out. And by the time I'd get back to that ol' first grade, everybody would be so far ahead of me, I'd give up till the next year. But comes September, if I'm anywhere near a school, I'll try again. Miss Bessie's convinced me it's worth while."

"Didn't anybody try to make you stay before?"

"They tried. But Pa didn't believe in it either." Then he laughed. "Want to hear something? One time an ol' man from the county office came out to the farm and asked how come I didn't go to school. And Pa brought out the shotgun and asked what business it was of anybody's whether I ever went to school." Skinny laughed so much he could hardly finish the story. "That ol' man took off like he'd been sent for," he concluded. "Pa was funny. Too bad he's dead."

"What about your mother?"

"She died a long time ago," answered Skinny. "I just barely remember her." He moved a rocker and swept behind it. "And that makes me an orphan," he continued. "Did you know that? I'm supposed to go and live in an orphans' home if they find one that'll have me."

One of the other highway men had come onto the porch. He patted Skinny on the head. "Why, this hotel would close up if you went chasing off to an orphans' home. Don't you run the place?"

"No," Skinny answered, "I just help out. I'd like to stay, but Miss Bessie only took me in so I'd have a place to live till something else comes along."

Two more highway workers came out of the hotel, and one of them said, "Back to work, men!"

The one who had been there longest complained, "There ought to be a law against working in July." He folded his newspaper and tossed it into the swing.

Skinny asked, "What about the weather forecast?"

The man pointed a finger at him. "Miss Bessie's right: schooling is worth while," he said, and followed the other men from the porch.

Skinny took his broom and started inside. "I hope it don't rain," he said under his breath. "I sure hope it don't rain tonight."

In the kitchen, Peachy was grumbling. "I wishes those highway men would take to coming to lunch on time. I got enough to do without cleaning up this kitchen twice."

"Have you seen a can of patching tar?" Skinny asked.

"I got enough to do without looking for a can of tar," said Peachy. "And besides, you're supposed to be bringing me them dirty dishes."

"That's where I'm headed," said Skinny, picking up a large tray and going into the dining room. He filled the tray with plates and glasses and returned to the kitchen.

Roman, the Negro man who worked at the hotel, came in from the garden with a basket of tomatoes. Skinny asked, "Don't either one of you know where that can of tar is?"

Peachy stopped her dishwashing. "Child, why's you so worried about tar?"

"Because I can finish patching the front porch roof when I find it. Reckon you got it mixed up with a bucket of syrup and put it in the pantry?" He started into the storage room.

"Don't go messing around that pantry," said Peachy. "If I don't know the difference 'twixt a bucket of syrup and a can of tar, I got no business being head cook in this establishment."

Roman, busy spreading out the tomatoes on a shelf near the window, looked up. "I didn't realize you were the head cook, Peachy-gal," he said, winking at Skinny. "I been thinking all this time you were the *only* cook here."

Peachy said, "That makes me the head one," and went on with her work.

Skinny was always glad when Roman was around; things were apt to be livelier. And besides, Roman was his friend. Sometimes he felt closer to him than to 'most anybody alive. In a way, Miss Bessie had rescued both of them from trouble. She had bailed Roman out of the chain gang, freeing him to work for her as long as he didn't get in a scrape with the law. And Skinny had been taken in until there was space for him at the orphanage. They both had rooms off the hotel's back porch, and sometimes at night when the work was done the two of them would sit out in the yard and talk. Roman would tell of his adventures before he had gone to jail, and Skinny would tell about how things used to be when he and his Pa were sharecropping.

Peachy finished washing the dishes and began to hang up her dishrag and towels. Roman emptied the last tomato from his basket and started toward the back door. "You better go ahead and check in the pantry," he said to Skinny. "Otherwise Peachy's liable to feed us hot biscuits some morning with patching tar poured over them." He closed the screen door behind him, and Peachy muttered that she had enough to do without worrying about sassy ex-convicts.

Skinny went to the front of the hotel and climbed to the roof by way of a trellis at the end of the porch. The roll of roofing was still there from the afternoon before, but he couldn't remember where he had put that worrisome can of tar. He was scratching his head to help him think, just as the doorbell rang.

Instead of climbing down to answer it, he crossed the roof to the edge nearest the front door. Lying on his stomach, he leaned his head over to see who was there. "Howdy," he called to the man and woman who stood nearby.

The couple looked around but did not see him. They glanced at each other. "I thought somebody spoke to us," said the man.

"It was me," said Skinny, pushing his head a little farther through the wisteria vine that ran along the top of the porch. He smiled at the couple and said, "Welcome to this-here hotel. Is there something I can do for you?" Before they could answer, Skinny pointed toward the trunk of a sweet gum tree. "Say," he said, "there's that can of tar I've been looking all over for." He asked the man, "Would you mind handing it up to me?"

The man went into the yard, took the can to the top

step, and held it over his head. "Thank you," said Skinny, reaching for the tar. "Now I'll come down and see what you're wanting."

He crossed the roof to the far end, climbed down the trellis, and jumped onto the porch. Instead of going across it he went into an end door and hurried to the back hall. He lifted his white jacket from the nail near the broom closet and put it on carefully, making certain the sleeves were turned back far enough for his hands to stick out. The bottom of the jacket struck him just above his knees, and his overalls were rolled up to just below them. Barefooted still, he walked to the front door.

He greeted the couple as if he were seeing them for the first time. "Howdy," he said, smiling hospitably. "Welcome to this-here hotel." Noticing the man looking at his coat, he explained, "It's my uniform. Somebody left it in one of the rooms and never did come back for it." He took a step or two across the porch and turned around, showing off the jacket from all sides.

The woman asked crossly, "May we see the manager?"

"The manager?"

"That's right."

"Oh," Skinny said, "we don't have a manager. This hotel ain't all that big."

"Somebody must run it," said the woman.

"Sure. Miss Bessie runs it. Would you care to see her?"

"Yes, please."

"She's not here," Skinny said. "But if you'll just take a seat, she'll be back before long." He motioned toward two rocking chairs for them, and he sat down in the swing. "Hot today, ain't it?" he said, when everyone was settled. The couple said nothing, and after a brief silence Skinny held out the newspaper. "Do you go in for reading?" he asked.

"We've read it," said the man.

Skinny flipped through a few of the pages, stopping from time to time as if he had come across an article of special interest. Then he put the paper down and said, "I was patching the roof when I heard the door-bell."

The man said, "You don't look big enough to be patching a roof."

Skinny stopped swinging and held his shoulders back and puffed out his chest as best he could. "I'm older than I look," he said. The couple didn't comment, and he went back to swinging, saying softly, "It's just that I'm not filled out good yet."

The woman asked, "Do you know if this Miss Bessie whatever-her-name-is will have a room to rent when she gets back?"

Skinny jumped to his feet. "Is that all you want? Why, I can rent you a room." He sat back down and asked solemnly, "Have you got two dollars and twenty-five cents?"

"Of course," said the man and reached for his wallet.

"Pay when you leave," said Skinny, leading the way into the hotel. "I just wanted to make sure you understood about that part." He explained as they followed him up the stairs that the price included supper and breakfast for both of them, and that they were in luck on account of this was chicken night. "Tuesdays are nice too," he said. "That's when we have pork chops." He pushed one door open as they went past. "This is the bathroom, but wait till nearer suppertime if you plan to bathe. There'll be hot water then."

The woman groaned. "None earlier?"

"The tank's hooked up to the cookstove," Skinny said. "But we start a fire about four-thirty." He led them into a room at the end of the hall, walked across it, and pulled up the shades to give more light. "It's pretty, ain't it?"

"Looks clean," said the woman, and the man agreed. "It's all right."

"Well," said Skinny, "have a seat"—motioning toward the chairs, while he sat down on the edge of the bed.

The couple looked at him, and the woman said, "That will be all, thank you."

"You're welcome," said Skinny, crossing his legs.

The man reached in his pocket. "I suppose you're waiting for a tip."

"No, sir," said Skinny. "We don't go in much for that. I just thought I'd catch you up on what's going on around here."

"We're not interested," the woman said. "Our car broke down and we're forced to spend the night. So if you would just—"

The man interrupted her. "Take this for your trouble," he told Skinny and held out a dime.

"I couldn't do that," said Skinny, reaching into his own pocket. "But I reckon I could accept a nickel." He took the dime that was offered him and counted out five pennies from his own change and gave them to the man.

He left then and went out to the chicken yard and gathered the eggs. That was one of his chores. Next he returned to the job of patching the roof. As he was pouring tar along a seam of it, he came near the window of the room the couple had rented. The man was saying, "That boy was going to tell us what was going on around here." After a sigh, he added, "What could be going on in this dried-up town?"

Skinny called out cheerily, "A watermelon-cutting."

The man stepped to the window and asked, "What'd you say?"

"The Baptists are having a watermelon-cutting tonight," Skinny said. "All you can eat for fifteen cents."

He took the can of patching tar and continued along the seam. "I ain't never been turned loose with all the watermelon I could eat," he called from across the roof. "Yes siree, this is going to be my big night!"

2 ꞌꞌꞌꞌꞌꞌꞌ *The Watermelon-cutting*

Skinny took the big bell from the dining room and
went upstairs. He rang it as he walked along, calling,
"Suppertime! Come to supper!" Downstairs he rang it
as he passed the parlor, and the guests there began to
rise. He opened the screen door that led to the front
porch, clanged the bell once more, and announced
loudly, "SUPPER'S SERVED!"

Two of the highway engineers and Miss Clydie Essex, the town's beauty-parlor operator, were seated at

the end of the porch. Miss Clydie didn't board at the hotel but ate supper there one night a week when she kept evening hours at her shop. One of the men said to Skinny, "Were you talking to us or to somebody across the street?"

The other one asked, "What'd you say, anyhow?"

"I said, 'Supper's served,' " Skinny explained. "It means supper's ready, that's all it means. I've heard tell that's the way they say it in city hotels."

The group walked across the porch. One man said, "In city hotels the dining room is open 'most all the time, and folks go in and out and order whatever they please."

Skinny sniffed. "Seems like a poor arrangement," he said, holding the door open for the trio to enter. "How do they know how many to fix for?"

Miss Clydie Essex said, "Pay him no mind, Skinny. I've been in some of those big hotels and the food's not near as good as it is here."

"Why, thank you, Miss Clydie," said Skinny. He started to bow to her as she walked inside, but one of the men gave a friendly poke at his stomach and he had to jump back.

After the blessing Roman passed hot biscuits and brought out extra platters of food, and Skinny began asking guests what they would like to drink. "Butter-milk, sweet milk, or iced tea?" When he received orders for as many glasses as he could handle, he would go to the kitchen. When he came to the couple who had arrived that day, he asked, "Buttermilk, sweet milk, or iced tea?" and the woman answered, "Coffee."

"Oh, we don't have coffee in the summertime," Skinny said. "Most folks like something cold."

"Well, I don't."

"We have coffee for breakfast," Skinny said proudly. "Every morning we have it."

The woman said, "Well, I'd like some now."

Miss Bessie, who had been chatting with the people at her table, looked across and asked, "Is something wrong?"

Skinny said, "I was just explaining that we don't have coffee at night."

Miss Bessie smiled at the woman. "That's right," she said. Then she added, "Except when we have fish. I think fish calls for coffee, no matter how hot the weather gets."

A man sitting near her said that he thought so too, and Miss Bessie turned back to her table. A discussion was soon under way about all the fish caught recently at Shallow Creek by local men.

Skinny stood very straight, holding his shoulders back so far that his white coat almost fell off. He said to the woman who was displeased about the choice of drinks, "Buttermilk, sweet milk, or iced tea?"

"Water," the woman answered, and Skinny quickly brought her a large glass of it filled with chunks of ice.

When supper was over he hurried along with his chores. "Ain't the knives and forks scrubbed yet?" he asked, agitating for Peachy to get on with the dish-washing. "How can I set the tables for tomorrow without knives and forks?" Most nights he wasn't in a rush to be finished with the after-supper chores. But most nights he wasn't going to a watermelon-cutting afterward.

Peachy sighed. "It's too hot a night to rush, child."

Roman, who was stacking away clean saucers, said, "Ain't no hotter than it was during your Revival Week." He was reminding her that the dishwashing was not likely to be as drawn-out when she was in a hurry to get away.

"One of these times you're gonna say the wrong thing," said Peachy, lowering her voice. "And all of a sudden I'll pick up this pan and empty the dish water right in your face."

Roman and Skinny laughed. Miss Bessie, at the ice-box rearranging shelves, asked, "What's so funny?"— but nobody could remember.

At last the dishwashing picked up to almost Revival Week speed, and the work was soon finished. Peachy took off her apron and went home; Roman went to the back porch, saying he would stay awake and listen out for guests who might need anything; and Miss Bessie and Skinny walked across town to the watermelon-cutting.

At the entrance to the long walkway in front of the Baptist church, they paid their admission fee to Mrs. Spunky Edison. She put the money into a cigar box she held in her lap. Miss Bessie looked toward the people gathered farther up the walk and in the pine grove to one side of it. "Seems like a good turnout," she said.

"All the Baptists," replied Mrs. Edison, "and half the Methodists."

Miss Trudy Boylan, who was assisting in taking up the money, added, "And we expect the other half of them when their choir practice lets out."

Skinny and Miss Bessie went on up the walk. "Reckon they planned for this big a crowd?" asked Skinny, sounding worried. "What if they run out of watermelons?"

Miss Bessie assured him there would be plenty. On a hot summer night, with nothing else going on in the community except the choir practice at the church across town, the Baptists naturally expected a lot of people.

"I hope so," Skinny said, "because my system sure is craving watermelon."

"I think it would be all right if you just said you were hungry for watermelon," suggested Miss Bessie.

"That's a good idea," Skinny agreed as they reached the edge of the crowd. "Goodness me!" he said. "It's as light as day out here." And he stopped to admire the extension lights that were swung from branches of the trees.

Miss Bessie told him to walk around and have himself a good time; she said she believed she would go over and visit with the ladies.

Mr. Barton Grice, the superintendent of the Sunday school, saw Skinny and asked if he wouldn't like to go across the yard and join in the games.

"No, sir," said Skinny, "I don't care too much for games."

Mr. Grice smiled. "All the children are there. Wouldn't you like to play with them?"

"No, sir," said Skinny. "I don't care too much for children." He didn't explain that he had never known other children very well and had seldom played with them.

A moment later one of the teachers he knew from Sunday school came over. "Come on, Skinny," she said. "Join in the fun."

"Thank you," said Skinny, "but I think I'll just stand around."

"Of course you won't," said the woman goodnaturedly. She put her hand on his neck and urged him forward to where the children were playing.

He recognized members of his Sunday-school class and soon was enjoying the game. It was " 'Tis but a Simpleton," and he was first to figure it out. He guessed right off what was required in order not to be a simpleton.

Next a game of "Cross Questions and Crooked Answers" got under way. One of the teachers from the Junior Department handed out questions on slips of paper to all the boys, and the girls were given answers. The boys stood on one side and the girls on the other.

The player at the head of each line stepped to the center, and the game began. The boy's question was: "Who was the first President of the United States?" The girl read her answer, which turned out to be: "I prefer pumpkin pie." They went through it three times. The boy remained solemn, but the girl giggled, so they both had to go to the ends of their lines.

The next question read was: "Shall I sing you a song?" and the answer was: "Underneath a washpot." Everybody laughed, including the two who were having their turn. They were sent to the ends of the lines, and the game continued.

Skinny was having a good time, and it would soon be his turn in the center. Then he realized that there he was, with his slip of paper—and not able to read what was on it. He thought of asking somebody to tell him what it said. But after he had won the last game himself, and everybody had said how smart he was to figure it out, this was no time to admit a weakness—even something as unimportant as not knowing how to read.

He kept his place in line and, when his turn came,

stepped to the center to meet the girl across from him. He looked down at the paper and, pretending to read, said, "Who was the *second* President of the United States?"

The girl snickered. Skinny wondered if it had been a mistake for him to make up a question. The girl then began to giggle hysterically.

The teacher said, "Why, Cloris, you laughed before you even read your answer. Scoot to the end of the line." Then she added, "But I don't think it was quite fair to Skinny. Shouldn't he have another chance?"

The players agreed, and the woman handed him a piece of paper. "Here's another question," she said.

"Thank you," said Skinny, smiling as he accepted it.

"Now just stay in the center," continued the woman. "And, let's see, it's Lora's turn from the girls' side."

At that a pretty thin-faced girl came forward, and everyone waited quietly for Skinny to read the question. Suddenly his face turned red and beads of perspiration appeared at the top of his forehead. He clenched his fists and cleared his throat but said nothing.

The teacher asked, "Is something wrong?"

"No, ma'am," said Skinny. He hesitated. "It's just that—I mean—" And then his eyes brightened and he pointed toward the walkline. "There's a boy over yonder who got here late," he said. "I don't feel right about reading so many questions when he hasn't had a one." He called out, "Howdy, over there! You can take my place if you want to."

The boy quickly accepted, asking as he took the question, "Are you tired of playing?"

"Yes," said Skinny, walking away, "I'd rather stand around." He went near a gathering of grown people and stood by himself.

Mr. Grice walked across to him. "You look worried, young man. What's on your mind?"

Skinny didn't like to talk about not knowing how to read and write. "I was just thinking," he said. "I mean I was sort of concerned about where the watermelons are. I don't see any here."

"Oh," said Mr. Grice, "they're at the icehouse—a truckload of 'em. They'll be brought over now directly."

Before Skinny could reply, Mr. Murray Huff came to speak to them. He owned the land where Skinny and his father had been sharecroppers until the old man died. "Well, Skinny-boy!" said Mr. Huff, sort of half chuckling, "with your face washed and clean clothes on I almost didn't know you. You're looking better."

"Yes, sir," said Skinny. "I think I do very well."

The men laughed, and Mr. Huff said, "I was out at the old place today."

"Who lives there now?" Skinny asked.

"Nobody. I can't find anybody worth a cuss, so I'm

gonna store corn in the house. That's about all it's fit for."

"Why, it's a fine place," said Skinny, shocked to hear such a comment about the house that had been his home until two months ago. Then he smiled, as a thought occurred to him. "I'll make a crop for you," he said.

Mr. Huff laughed, but Skinny continued, "I could do it. I ain't awful big, but I'm strong." He rushed on as if he were sure the plan would work out if he put it in words soon enough. "If you'd just get me up a mule and stake me to a few supplies, you'd be plumb surprised at what all I can do."

When he stopped, Mr. Huff laughed more and didn't even comment on the idea. Instead he asked, "Remember that little rat-terrier-looking dog you used to have?"

"Sure," said Skinny. "That was R. F. D."

This time it was Mr. Grice who laughed. "How'd a dog get a name like that?"

"On account of the mailman gave him to me. R. F. D. stands for Rural Free Delivery. Did you know that?"

"I'd heard it," said Mr. Grice, and Skinny continued, "Pa wasn't feeling well one night and ran him off. Threw rocks at that poor dog and chased him into the woods. I tried to find him but couldn't."

"Your pa was a mite cantankerous at times," said Mr. Huff.

"No, sir," said Skinny, "he wasn't cantankerous. He just didn't feel well sometimes. But I genuinely hated for him to chase off R. F. D."

"Well," said Mr. Huff, "what I set out to tell you was that the dog has turned up again. He was sitting on the back steps when I drove up today. I didn't throw a rock at him, but he lit out for the woods so fast you'd have thought I did."

"What?" Skinny said. "He's back? I always figured Pa hurt him worse than he meant to and drove him to take up with somebody else."

"He better take up with somebody else," said Mr. Huff, " 'cause there sho ain't nobody out there now."

"No, sir," agreed Skinny, "there sho ain't. And I'm obliged to you for telling me you saw him." He started away from the two men then but, instead of going toward the crowd, turned and walked in the opposite direction.

At the end of the walkway Mrs. Edison was collecting admission money from latecomers. She noticed Skinny and asked, "Aren't you staying for the cutting?"

"No, ma'am," answered Skinny, heading into the dark. "I don't crave watermelon as much as I thought I did."

3 ꞋꞋꞋꞋꞋꞋꞋ R.F.D.

"The first time I seen the boll weevil,
   He was sitting on the square.
 The next time I seen the boll weevil,
   He had all his family there.
 He was looking for a home, just a-looking for a home."

Skinny told himself he was singing to keep awake and
that it had nothing to do with his being out by himself
in the middle of the night, a good three miles from the

nearest living soul. He sang the verse again as he made his way along the dirt road, and afterward said aloud— just to keep awake—"Boll weevil, you ain't got nothing on me. I'm a-looking for a home too."

Then he admitted to himself he wasn't exactly looking for a home tonight. He was looking for a dog, and the thought that cheered him was that he might find R. F. D.

As for his finding a home, he wasn't too worried. He liked helping out at the hotel and wished he could just stay on there. It would be all right with him if the orphanage decided not to take him. Maybe now that he was about to find R. F. D. a problem would be set up that would work in his favor. He'd send word to the orphanage that he wouldn't care to join them if his dog couldn't come along. And if they sent word back, "No dogs," well, he would settle down to a job at the hotel. And that would be the end of that. Except, of course, Miss Bessie might not take to the idea. But Roman and Peachy were sure to be on his side and, between the three of them, they could out-talk Miss Bessie.

He was thinking how nice it was going to be, when all of a sudden a sound from the creek nearby reminded him that he was in the open country. "Good for you, Froggie!" he called. "Town frogs can't make near that much noise."

The sound came again, and Skinny affected a deep, croaky voice. *"Jug-o'-rum* to you too," he answered and went on his way, singing the ballad that was on his mind.

Again he compared himself to the boll weevil, saying under his breath, "The boll weevil always flourished, no matter where he went." He called out loud, "If you can do it, boll weevil, so can I," and sang another of the verses to give himself heart:

"The farmer took the boll weevil
   And froze him in a chunk of ice.
The boll weevil said to the farmer,
   'This is mighty cool and nice,
This will be my home, this will be my home.' "

He walked for a long way through a wooded area. Coming out onto the property owned by the Whitfield Dairy, he decided to take a short cut across the pasture lands—it would save a lot of walking. He climbed over the fence and made his way down the grassy hillside, through the marshy bottoms, and up the other side. He did not sing now because he needed to listen for trouble. In the daytime he had been chased across the pasture by a Jersey bull on more than one occasion. Since he did not know if the bull was penned up nights, it would be smart not to risk a sneak attack. So he kept an eye out for anything moving and an ear out for strange noises and his mind on what he was doing.

At the opposite fence line he climbed out of the pasture and onto the trail. It led to the house that had been home to him. One more mile and he would be there.

He could tell the difference in the air already and believed that if he were blindfolded and plunked down in this very spot he would know where he was. It had that special smell to it—clear and cool, and crab-appley, even when the trees were not in bloom. It was the lowest spot nearby, and in the center of the crab-apple thicket there was the finest spring of cold water anywhere. That reminded him, he was thirsty.

He left the trail and went along a footpath into the thicket. At the spring he found the gourd dipper he and his father had put there for drinking purposes, and dipped it into the cool water. After drinking two dip-perfuls, he was returning the gourd to a rock nearby when a slithering streak caused him to jump back. Then he heard a splash. "A snake! In mine and Pa's drinking hole!" he said disgustedly, and went away thinking discouraging thoughts.

He began whistling when he came in sight of the house. Nearer, he called, "Here, R. F. D. Come on, pup. Come on, boy." But the dog was not to be seen.

At the house Skinny stood in the yard and for a long time called and whistled in every direction. Then he went to the barn and tried from there. "Come on, pup. Come on now. It's me, Skinny, and I ain't gonna throw a rock at you. I ain't never thrown a rock at you, you know that."

But the dog did not appear, and Skinny went back to the house, called one last time, and went inside. Maybe after sunrise he could locate R. F. D.

In the little bit of moonlight that came in through the windows, he pulled together a few burlap bags that were in the room and lay down. He was not sleepy, tired as he was. It was a strange feeling to be back here and to know that the house was empty except for him. Twice he heard scratching noises and ran and opened the door, expecting to find R. F. D. there. The first time he decided the noise had been made by a sycamore limb brushing against the corner of the house. The second time he decided it wasn't even a limb, but just his imagination, and walked back to his burlap bags and went to sleep.

In the morning he began to wake up when sunlight came in through the window. One eye opened just enough to see the rafters overhead, and in his half-asleep state he forgot that things had changed. "Pa," he called, stretching his arms and legs, "wake up, Pa, it's daybreak." He was on his feet, stretching again, before he remembered that he was alone in the house.

He went to the front door and looked out at the yard. The weeds had grown higher, but nothing else had changed. Then he crossed to the back window. The castor beans had come up again this year and were so tall they hid the hayrack. His eyes wandered next to the site of the old woodpile, and he straightened up with a start. There was R. F. D., scratching dirt from around the chopping block. Skinny rushed to the door and called, "R. F. D.! Come here, boy!"

But the dog ran off the other way and was soon hidden on the far side of the barn. Skinny headed in that direction, then changed his mind. The best thing to do would be to wait. It was taking a chance, he knew, but it was the only way. If he chased R. F. D., the dog could easily outrun him, so he went back to the steps of the house, sat down, and began to whistle.

After a few minutes the dog ventured a few steps from the barn. "Come on," called Skinny. "It's just me." And he coaxed until the dog was almost to the woodpile. "Stop and dig for a rat if you want to. I'll wait for you," he said, watching R. F. D. come closer and closer. He tried not to appear too anxious and leaned back to rest his elbow on the step behind him. But his elbow struck an empty bucket that had been left there, knocking it to the ground with a clattering noise. R. F. D. turned and ran all the way past the barn and disappeared in a clump of pokeweed.

Skinny had to begin all over. "Come on, R. F. D.," he called. "Come on, pup. It's just me, ol' Skinny, sitting here."

At last R. F. D. came out of his hiding place. He took a few steps toward the house and sat down, then started off again and got as far as the woodpile. He stopped and sniffed the chopping block and turned and headed back in the opposite direction. After a few steps he turned again and slowly made his way toward the house. Skinny continued to whistle but otherwise was as still as could be. When R. F. D. was a few feet away he seemed all at once to remember his old friend. He hopped onto the steps and put his head against Skinny's leg.

"You done gone wild," said Skinny, patting the dog on the back and head. "Did you know that?" He lifted him onto his lap and leaned over so that his cheek touched R. F. D.'s forehead. "But I'm glad to see you anyhow."

After a few more minutes of getting used to each other, they set out for town. Skinny kept looking back at the house until it was out of sight. Then he concentrated on telling R. F. D. what town life was like. After that they came to the short cut through the pasture, and he concentrated on watching out for the Jersey bull. At the marshy bottom land he couldn't do much watching because of the dense undergrowth.

Soon they came onto open pasture again—and there stood the bull. Skinny thought of turning back, but it would be a shame to waste the time. So he remained very still, and the bull looked at him. Finally it went back to grazing on the clover that grew there, and Skinny decided the time had come to make a break for the road ahead.

He and R. F. D. struck out across the pasture as fast as they could run, not looking back to see if they were being chased. At the fence, R. F. D. shot under it and Skinny bounded over it. And the bull, who had not stirred from across the way, continued to graze in the clover patch.

The dirt road through the woods came out at the highway, and the highway led to town. Skinny and R. F. D. had been walking for more than an hour when two lumber trucks passed them. The first one kept going, but the second one stopped. A man sitting in the cab with the driver called, "Want a lift?"

Skinny caught R. F. D. up in his arms and climbed onto the logs that were chained to the long trailer. "We're on," he called, and the truck drove away.

At the "Stop" sign near the hotel, he scrambled to the ground, told the driver, "Much obliged for the ride," and started toward Miss Bessie's. Holding onto R. F. D., he apologized. "It's just that I don't want you taking any notion to run off."

He cut through the side yard and before he was beyond the scuppernong arbor heard Peachy at the kitchen window announcing his arrival. Miss Bessie was on the back porch before he got to the steps, wanting to know where he had been. She told him she had been worried sick-to-death and that she was responsible for his well-being. She asked him please not to cause her such concern again. Then she wanted to know what they needed with a dog.

"He's the best ratter you ever did see," said Skinny. "I felt like I'd be letting you down if I didn't go fetch him."

"We don't have rats," said Miss Bessie.

"Then I'll teach him to be a watchdog. It wouldn't surprise me if he don't turn out to catch burglars right and left."

Miss Bessie smiled. "We don't have burglars, either. But I guess you can keep him."

"Thank you," said Skinny. "I appreciate it. And I want you to know that he's an outdoors dog. Only I'm afraid he might run off at first, and if you wouldn't mind—"

Miss Bessie interrupted him. "You can keep him in the hotel," she said, and Skinny hurried inside.

In the kitchen he received another scolding from Peachy. But he could tell she was glad he was back, even though she went on grumbling. "I done peeled all the potatoes myself, and shucked the corn, and mopped the dining room, and done all the things you're supposing to."

"I'll make it up to you," said Skinny. "I'll churn for you. Has the milk clabbered yet?"

"I done that too." Peachy sighed.

"Then I'll wash dishes today and tomorrow and you can just sit around and rest."

Peachy's voice wasn't grumbly now and she said, "No, child, I don't want you to wash the dishes. I just wants you not to run off no more."

Before Skinny could answer, they heard Miss Bessie calling from the back yard. "Bring some knives and a saltcellar," she told Peachy, "and you and Skinny come on out here."

In the back yard Roman was setting a big watermelon on the bench usually occupied by the washtubs. Miss Bessie explained to Skinny. "Without you there last night, they had more than they knew what to do with. So I sent Roman down to the icehouse this morning to buy one of the leftovers."

Skinny stepped up to the bench and thumped the watermelon. "It's just exactly ripe," he said, and Roman agreed with him. Peachy thumped it too and pronounced it "a little on the green side." Roman told her she was crazy as a bedbug.

Before they had a chance to argue Miss Bessie cut the melon, and each of them ate a quarter of it. They agreed that in hot weather nothing could beat cold watermelon. They also agreed that this was one of the best they had ever tasted—except Peachy thought it could have been a shade riper.

Skinny asked if the man and woman who had arrived the afternoon before had checked out.

"They left right after breakfast," Roman answered. "And guess how much coffee the woman drank."

"A gallon?" Skinny guessed.

"No," said Roman. "Half a cup."

Skinny and Miss Bessie laughed, but Peachy muttered, "And I made a whole extra measurement of it on account of her."

They finished eating the watermelon and hacked up the rinds for the three cows Miss Bessie owned. Roman piled the scraps into a bucket and set out toward the barn. Peachy gathered up the knives and was rinsing them under the back-yard faucet when the doorbell rang.

"I'll go," said Skinny, hurrying up the steps. "I ain't done nothing all morning." He called as he went through the kitchen, "Come on, R. F. D., I'll show you how we answer the door." He rushed ahead, snatching his white coat off the nail by the broom closet and pulling it on over his overalls. He arrived at the front door out of breath.

"Howdy," he said, seeing the almost-elderly gentleman who stood there. "Welcome to this-here hotel." He noticed then what the man was wearing: patent-leather shoes, white pants, a striped coat, and one of those flat-top straw hats.

Skinny usually opened the screen door and took a few steps onto the porch. Callers could then see his white coat and be impressed by it. This time he forgot his own appearance and, followed by R. F. D., circled around to the other side of the visitor. With admiration in his voice, he said, "Them's the finest-looking garments I ever saw."

"Thank you kindly," said the man, with a smile so broad that gold teeth in the back of his mouth glistened in the sunlight. "And I'll just return the compliment. You're done up sporty yourself."

"What's your name?" asked Skinny.

"I can't recollect, offhand, what my name is," said the gentleman. "But my friends call me Daddy Rabbit."

4 ''''''''' *The Carnival and Calvin*

It turned out that the caller's real name was Frank J. Rabbit. He explained to Miss Bessie, who had come onto the porch, "I'm older than most of our construction crew, and the young bucks got started calling me Daddy Rabbit."

Skinny's eyes lit up, and he laughed. "That's a good

one," he said, and, seeing that Miss Bessie and the gentleman didn't think it was all that funny, he added, "Young bucks, buck rabbits. Get it?"

"Yeah," said the man happily. "I made a joke and didn't know it." He turned back to Miss Bessie and explained that he was with an engineering crew beginning the new bridge over Flint River. Most of his co-workers had found rooms in Vickstown. "But the hotel there has filled up," he said. "So I drove over here to see if you might have space for three of us."

Miss Bessie asked, "Where are the other two?"

"They're on the job. I was elected to scout around for rooms."

"Come in," said Miss Bessie, "and I'll show you what we have."

After Daddy Rabbit had looked at the rooms and found them to his liking he began to unload his car. "I'll bring up your suitcases," said Skinny, insisting that everything be left to him. There were three bags, and by the time he got upstairs with the second one, Daddy Rabbit was busy unpacking the first.

"Don't wear yourself out," said Daddy Rabbit. "Set a spell before you haul up the last one."

"I'll just do that," said Skinny. He wasn't tired, but the clothes that were being unpacked looked interesting. He thought he might as well watch. Taking a seat near the bureau, he asked, "What's it like to work on a construction crew?"

Daddy Rabbit stopped what he was doing. "It's jim-dandy," he said enthusiastically. "You get to move around and meet new folks all the time. I wouldn't have my life any other way." He added, "No sir, it's the only life for me," and went back to his unpacking. He transferred socks to the dresser drawer from a suitcase and then lifted out a batch of ties.

Skinny said, "Those are sure colorful neckties."

Daddy Rabbit held them at arm's length. "Struck by a rainbow," he said admiringly, "and they're for every day. Wait till you see my Sunday ones!"

Skinny went to get the last suitcase and, when he had brought it up, sat down again. Daddy Rabbit reached into his pocket. "I better tip you, hadn't I?" he said.

"That's not what I'm waiting for," Skinny explained. "I just thought I'd tell you what all's going on around here."

"Good," said Daddy Rabbit, sitting down in a chair across the room.

"Well," said Skinny, "now that you mention it, not anything is going on. The Baptists had a watermelon-cutting, but that was last night. And there was an all-day singing out at Pine Crossing two Sundays ago." He got up to leave. "But things do happen from time to time," he added, not sounding at all certain that anything would.

Daddy Rabbit smiled. "It appears that I know more

about the activity in these parts than you do. For instance, I saw something interesting when we drove through Vickstown this morning."

"That's fourteen miles away," Skinny said.

"Just a nice little drive," said Daddy Rabbit, as if automobile travel were in everybody's power. "And do you know that they have a carnival set up over there?"

"Is that right?" said Skinny. "I've heard of carnivals." Then he decided not to be too impressed by what Vickstown had to offer. "We had a tent movie over here a while back," he said. "Too bad you missed it."

"Why, I've seen more picture shows than you can shake a stick at," Daddy Rabbit said. He went on to say that there wasn't anything more fun than a carnival.

"I've never been to one," Skinny said. "But I've seen six moving pictures. The week the tent was here Miss Bessie gave me money enough to go every night. What do you think of that?"

"I think there's nothing like a carnival," said Daddy Rabbit, and Skinny decided he had better be getting downstairs.

Daddy Rabbit handed him a quarter as he started out. "Thank you," said Skinny, "but I don't have any change."

"The quarter is for you."

"I can't take that much," Skinny said. "But a nickel or a dime would be all right. You can owe it to me if you don't have one handy."

Daddy Rabbit said, "Then help me get these suitcases back downstairs." He took a pair of trousers that he had just unpacked and began to fold them. "I refuse to stay at any hotel where I can't tip as much as I please."

Skinny didn't know what to say and decided he'd better take the quarter.

Daddy Rabbit said, "Now I have to go out to the new job." He snapped his heels together and bowed. "I'm pleased to have made your acquaintance," he added. "And I'll see you at suppertime."

Late in the afternoon Roman reported that one of the cows had not returned to the barn at feeding time. He asked if Skinny would help hunt for it.

The pasture was large, as town pastures went. Most families in the community kept their cows in grazing lots, but Miss Bessie owned enough land to have a sizable pasture. Skinny started down one side of it, and Roman checked the other. They met at the far end. Neither had seen the missing cow—nor a broken place in the fence where she might have got out.

"Then she's in here somewhere," said Roman, and

they split up again to continue the search. After a while Skinny heard Roman calling to him from a clump of pine saplings.

The cow had given birth to a calf, and both were resting on the straw-covered ground. Skinny patted the calf, and it got to its feet. "It's solid red, I do believe," he said, walking around to the other side of it. "No, here's a white spot on one leg."

"He's not too wobbly," said Roman. "Must have been born this morning." He tapped the cow on her back to make her stand up. "We better take 'em to the barn."

By the time the cow and calf had been driven to the barn and bedded down for the night, supper in the hotel was over. Peachy grumbled when Roman and Skinny came into the kitchen. "Me and Miss Bessie did all the work by ourselves," she complained, not at all impressed with the report of a new calf. "And besides the regular crowd, there was that there Daddy Rabbit and them two other bridge-builders he brung back."

Roman told her that he and Skinny had been working hard too and were powerful hungry.

Peachy said, "There ain't nothing left except cornbread and a little pot liquor from the turnip greens."

"Nothing left!" said Roman.

Skinny added, "And this was steak night!"

They sat down then, and Roman said it wouldn't be

the first time he had made a meal of cornbread and pot liquor. Skinny said he could remember plenty of nights in his life when he had not had any supper at all.

Peachy suddenly began to laugh. Then she opened the warming closet of the stove. "I just wanted to scare you," she said and handed them a platter containing a generous amount of country-fried steak and another of potatoes, baked squash, and stuffed eggplant. Next she brought out a bowl of Crowder peas and a plate of biscuits, and from the icebox a tray of sliced tomatoes and cucumbers.

All the while she laughed heartily. It was the most Skinny had heard her laugh since the time Moon Mullins got in such an awful argument with Lady Plushbottom. That happened in the funny papers. Peachy couldn't read either, but Roman could, and every morning he read the funnies aloud to Peachy and Skinny. It was an important event of each day.

Skinny and Roman finished their supper and got busy with the clearing up. Afterward, Skinny was walking through the front hall when Daddy Rabbit came down the stairs. "My young friends are tired out from their first day on the job," he said, referring to his coworkers who were staying at the hotel. "They're going to bed early, so why don't you just come with me to that carnival I told you about?"

"Me?" said Skinny. "Well, ain't that a good idea! I'll go ask Miss Bessie."

He went into the parlor, and Miss Bessie returned to the hall with him. "You won't be out late, will you, Mr. Rabbit?" she asked.

"Not if you'll come with us."

She smiled. "Thank you, but I have some sewing to do."

"It'll keep. Why don't you join us?"

Miss Bessie smiled again and said she hadn't been to a carnival in so many years she had forgotten what one was like. Daddy Rabbit told her that in that case it was high time she refreshed her memory and kept insisting that she come along. Five minutes later the three of them were off to Vickstown.

At the carnival Daddy Rabbit stepped up to the first tent they came to and bought three tickets to a flame-swallowing act. Skinny remained silent during the exhibition, but when it was over he said, "It's a wonder those folks don't burn their insides out."

"Made me plumb thirsty," said Daddy Rabbit. "Let's go drink us a Coke."

After refreshments Skinny rode on the swings and the Loop-o-Plane, while Daddy Rabbit and Miss Bessie waited for him. Then all three of them took in more side shows. One featured an exotic dancing girl who, the announcer said, came from old Trinidad. The girl whispered something to him, and he told the audience, "She comes from old Baghdad, but what's the difference? Both are far-off places."

At the shooting gallery Miss Bessie made the highest score. She hit five wooden ducks in a row and won a walking-stick for a prize. Daddy Rabbit called her "Deadeye" as they walked away laughing, agreeing that it was time to leave for home. It was already later than they had planned to stay.

"Let's have one last ride," suggested Daddy Rabbit. "What about the whip?"

"No, indeed," said Miss Bessie. "You two go ahead, and I'll just watch."

Daddy Rabbit bought only one ticket. Handing it to Skinny, he said, "We might be across the way when you finish." As Skinny left them, he heard Miss Bessie saying she guessed she wasn't too old to ride the Ferris wheel.

After the whip ride Skinny walked across and waited by the Ferris wheel. It spun by twice. Then there was a loud clunking noise and the wheel came to a halt. Daddy Rabbit and Miss Bessie were at the very top.

The woman who sold tickets came out of her booth and said to a boy standing nearby, "Get a move on you, Calvin! Help your pa!" To the people standing near she said, "Something went wrong with the mechanism. It'll be fixed in a minute." She went back to the booth, gathered up the money and tickets, and headed toward a row of tents.

The man working on the machinery called for the boy, Calvin, to hand him various tools. "Not that one, you dunce," he would say. "The other one." After a while he didn't call for anything else, and Calvin walked over to where Skinny was standing. He pointed toward the top of the Ferris wheel and asked, "You waiting for them?"

"Yes."

"Your ma and pa?"

"No," said Skinny. "I don't have no ma and pa."

Calvin's face brightened. "Well, ain't you lucky!" he said.

"No, I'm not lucky," said Skinny. "My folks are both dead."

"Well, I don't wish mine were dead, but they sure can be a hindrance." The man yelled then for a hammer, and Calvin hurried to deliver it. A moment later he was back. "How old are you?" he asked.

"Eleven," answered Skinny, "going on twelve." He swatted a mosquito that had landed on the back of his neck and continued, "I ain't especially big for my age."

Calvin looked at him. "You *are* kind of scrawny," he said, and Skinny frowned. Calvin was as thin as he was. "Stand up straight," commanded Calvin and stood with his back to Skinny's. He felt with one hand to see whose head was higher, then turned around and laughed. "Want to hear something funny?" he asked. "I'm already twelve, and I ain't as big as you are." They both laughed as if it were the best joke they'd heard in a long time.

Skinny asked, "How long, you think, before the Ferris wheel will be fixed?"

"Another hour or two."

"But the lady said it would be running in a few minutes."

Calvin shrugged. "That was Ma. She always says that." Then he asked, "Do you live in a real house?" When he heard about the hotel he wanted to know if it had an upstairs and a downstairs and were there steps from one to the other with a banister rail and all that. "I've never lived in a real house," he said sadly. Then his tone changed and he gave a forced-sounding laugh and said loudly, "Who cares about a real house?" and pointed toward the tents. "I have more fun than anybody. I visit the side shows whenever I please and I can go free on all the rides. Ain't that a heap better than what you got? Who cares about stair steps?" He looked at Skinny, who was saying nothing. His voice became softer and he continued, "Want to know something? I almost never go to the side shows, and there's only one ride that I like." He made a sweeping gesture to include the entire carnival. "I'm tired of everything here except the swings."

Skinny said, "I don't guess you've been troubled by too much schooling, have you?" He smiled politely. "I'm pleased to come across somebody who hasn't been sitting in a schoolhouse all his life."

"Oh, I've been to school," said Calvin, and Skinny's

smile disappeared. "We go to Florida when it gets cold and stay there till spring. I been to school plenty."

"You mean you can read and write?"

"Sure," said Calvin. "Everybody can read and write." He noticed Skinny's expression and asked, "Can't you?"

"No, I ain't never took it up."

Calvin didn't say what a terrible thing that was, or carry on about the importance of book-learning. He just scratched his elbow for a few seconds. Then he began telling about a time when the Ferris wheel broke down and didn't get started up again until the next morning. After that he looked Skinny in the eye and said, "You know what me and you ought to do? We ought to run away."

"Now?" asked Skinny.

"No. But sometime."

"Where would we run to?"

"Any place you think of," Calvin said. "I can't do all the planning."

"I don't know many places," said Skinny. "And besides, I'm not in favor of it." Then he added, sort of under his breath, "At least not till I find out for sure whether I've got to go to that orphanage." It was the first time he had admitted to anybody that he cared one way or the other about the prospect of going to the orphans' home.

Just then the Ferris wheel made a chugging noise

and, after several jerky starts, began to turn. In less than a minute Daddy Rabbit and Miss Bessie were stepping to the ground.

"What's it like being stuck up there?" Skinny asked.

"Mighty pleasant," Daddy Rabbit said, "mighty pleasant!" And Miss Bessie laughed. She put her hand on Skinny's shoulder and said, "Next time I'll ride the merry-go-round."

Skinny heard Miss Bessie call Daddy Rabbit "Frank" instead of "Mr. Rabbit" as they started off. And Daddy Rabbit called her "Bessie." There must have been time on the Ferris wheel for them to get better acquainted. It was nice that they were coming away from it on such a friendly basis.

He looked around and saw that Calvin was watching him walk off and went back to say good-by. "It was a genuine pleasure meeting up with you," he said.

"Listen," said Calvin, speaking softly so that his father would not overhear them. "If you ever decide on running away, look for me."

"I will," Skinny said. "I'll look for you—if I decide to run away."

5 ↑↑↑↑↑↑↑ The Trucks Roll into Town

Skinny and Roman were repairing the gate to Miss Bessie's chicken yard. R. F. D. was at their heels at first. Later he stretched out on the shady side of the henhouse and took a nap.

"Come on, pup," Skinny called when the gate was mended. "Let's go, boy." He called again, but the dog did not appear. After looking in every part of the yard, he and Roman walked down into the pasture. They called and whistled, but nothing happened.

They returned to the yard and Roman stopped at the woodpile to chop kindling. "That little country dog probably got tired of town life," he said, mopping perspiration from his face with a red and white bandanna. "And I don't blame him. If I had four legs and could track rabbits, I'd strike out for the woods too."

"I better go look for him," said Skinny and went into the hotel to speak to Miss Bessie. If he had to go all the way back to the farm, he didn't want her to be alarmed.

The door to Miss Bessie's room was partly open, and he called softly, "Miss Bessie?"

"Come in, Skinny," she answered, and he entered the room. She was sitting in a rocking chair, sewing scraps together for a patchwork quilt. "What is it?" she asked.

Before Skinny could say what was on his mind, there was a stirring on the other side of Miss Bessie's chair and R. F. D. came running out. "Why, he's here!" said Skinny. "He's what I was worried about."

"Didn't you put him inside?"

"No, ma'am," answered Skinny, looking puzzled. "Maybe Peachy let him in when she went to the store."

Miss Bessie reached down and patted R. F. D. "He looked at me from the hallway at first," she explained, "and then came in to see what I was up to." Just then R. F. D. lay down on the bag of pieces for the quilt.

"Get up, R. F. D.!" said Skinny. "Them's Miss Bessie's good scraps."

Miss Bessie laughed. "He won't hurt them. Why

don't you have a seat and rest too? Or maybe you'd rather scout around and find some boys to play with."

"No, thank you, ma'am," said Skinny. He always turned down this suggestion. The only person his own age he had ever felt very comfortable around was Calvin. Too bad the carnival was not nearby. Some of the town boys might be all right too, but the few times he had visited with them hadn't been much fun. The talk always got around to things that had happened at school at one time or another.

He said to Miss Bessie now, "Maybe when school starts I'll go back and really buckle down. And besides learning to read and write, I'll make me some friends." Then a frown came across his face. "If only I didn't have to start in the first grade." He shook his head. "You've got no idea how little the rest of them first-graders are."

Miss Bessie smiled. "They get smaller every year, don't they?"

"They sure do."

"That's because you get bigger. But when you get to the orphanage, I expect the teachers will help you catch up on the things you've missed." She picked up a scrap of cloth and trimmed its edges. "You'll probably skip a grade or two if you work as hard in your studies as you do in helping me run the hotel."

"Couldn't I maybe just stay on here?" asked Skinny eagerly. "I could work before school and in the afternoons too." Sounding even more urgent, he added, "Or I could help you full time." He shrugged. "It won't matter if I don't get my educating."

"Education," corrected Miss Bessie. "And it does matter that you go back to school. It will matter the rest of your life." She was so emphatic about it that Skinny nodded his head in agreement. If she said it was important, then it must be important.

"The preacher told me today that he thinks there'll be room for you in a few weeks at the church home in the mountains," Miss Bessie continued. "It's one of the best orphanages anywhere—with a school and everything right there."

Skinny looked away from her. "I sure don't look forward to leaving this hotel."

"If I were a married woman," said Miss Bessie, "I wouldn't let them take you away."

"Oh, it don't make no difference to me whether you're married or not."

"Thank you," said Miss Bessie, "but you'll be better off where there's a man around to help with your up-bringing. You'll get the attention you need." Smiling, she added, "And you won't have to worry about all those first-graders. You'll be around boys your own age most of the time."

Instead of being convinced that the orphanage was the solution to his problem, Skinny said, "Miss Bessie, we ought to get you up a husband."

Miss Bessie laughed. "Now that's a good idea!" she said, getting out of the rocker. "Come on, let's go make us a lemonade."

In the kitchen, Skinny chipped ice into an earthenware pitcher, then gazed out the window while Miss Bessie squeezed lemons. "It looks cold in the mountains," he said sadly. "Even on a hot day like this it looks cold up there." He glanced at Miss Bessie, who had added the lemon juice and sugar to the pitcher and was now filling it with water. "And it's such a long way off," he continued. "Ain't there an orphans' home nearer by?"

"It's only forty miles away," said Miss Bessie.

"Forty miles is a far piece," said Skinny, taking the glass that was offered him. The lemonade brightened his outlook immediately, and he was soon reporting on what a fine job he and Roman had done in repairing the chicken-yard gate.

"Call Roman," suggested Miss Bessie, "and see if he'd like some refreshment."

Roman came to the house, and Peachy got back from the store, and everybody drank lemonade until it was gone. Then they set about their chores; it would soon be suppertime.

After supper Skinny knew that Daddy Rabbit and Miss Bessie were in the parlor, and he was eager to finish the night's work and go visit with them. He wanted to hear the tales Daddy Rabbit would be telling of his experiences around the country. Peachy said, "If you're rushing to go sit in yonder"—motioning toward the front of the hotel—"it's my opinion that you ought to leave them by themselves."

"How come?" asked Skinny.

" 'Cause they likes each other. I can tell it in their eyes."

"Reckon they'll get married?"

"They ain't gonna do nothing," said Peachy, "as long as you sits in there supervising."

Roman, who was drying dishes, said, "Daddy Rabbit ain't gonna get married; he's too much of a traveling man to settle down." Imitating Peachy, he added, "I can see it in his eyes."

"Mind your own business," said Peachy, and Roman and Skinny laughed.

When the work was finished the three of them left the kitchen. Peachy went home and Roman walked across town. Skinny called R. F. D. and they sat on the back steps in the moonlight.

After a while Miss Bessie came out looking for him. She and Daddy Rabbit were going for a drive and wanted him to come along. He hopped to his feet, pleased to accept the invitation.

In the car, settled on the back seat with R. F. D. perched beside him, it crossed his mind that maybe he ought not to have come. Peachy would think it wasn't wise. But he had stayed out of the parlor, and he reckoned that was enough to begin with.

Daddy Rabbit reported that a carnival was coming to town the next week, but he doubted if it would be the same one they had seen in Vickstown. That one was probably off in another part of the state by now. Skinny was sorry. He wondered how Calvin was getting along and if he was still thinking of running away.

But on Sunday morning when the trucks began to roll into town, he was glad that a carnival was coming —same one or not. He ran back and forth to the yard, watching the heavy loads of equipment pass along the dirt road in front of the hotel. They were going to the public grounds at the edge of town. Peachy complained that he was not bringing the breakfast dishes to the kitchen fast enough. "How you gonna get to Sunday school if you don't get your work done?"

"I think I'll just skip Sunday school," said Skinny happily and hurried to the front door to see if anything new was in sight. A few minutes later he was back with a tray of plates he had cleared from the tables as he came through the dining room. "You should have seen that last one," he announced in the kitchen. "The merry-go-round was taken clean apart and piled onto a truck. One of the horses almost joggled off when they struck that bump out front."

Miss Bessie said, "I do wish the constable would

send the fire hose over to wet down the road. We'll be buried in dust with all the passing back and forth this week." Then she told Skinny that he could go watch for more trucks if the dishes were all out of the dining room, but that he would have to go to Sunday school when the time came. Skinny thought it wouldn't hurt to leave it off this time, but Miss Bessie said, "You won't miss much of the carnival crowd. They'll be straggling in all day."

He waited in the front yard for a long time, but nothing else came by so he went to his room off the back porch. There he changed into the clean pants and shirt Miss Bessie had got ready for him. Passing through the back hall, he put on his white coat and looked at himself in the mirror. He was pleased with the effect. The coat and clean shirt and pants made a fine combination. He turned around, looked at himself longer, then took off the coat. None of the other boys dressed up that much for Sunday school, and he guessed he wouldn't either.

Miss Bessie called, "Dampen my hair brush and bring it to me." He pretended not to hear, and she called louder, "If you don't, I may use the other side of it on you." He could tell that she was teasing him and dampened the brush and carried it to her, along with a comb. She parted his hair and slicked it back as best she could.

At Sunday school Skinny was the third one to arrive.

A short, heavy-set boy called Lard was there already, and a regular-sized one named Elmer. The talk was mostly about the carnival, and Skinny reported in detail on the trucks he had seen passing. He said that carnivals weren't anything new to him, however. Only a few weeks ago he had taken in the one over at Vickstown. Elmer had gone to that one also, and he and Skinny discussed the various rides and side shows. Lard said he hadn't got there because it had rained every time his family planned to go. He was hoping for a better streak of weather for the one here.

Soon other boys and girls began to arrive and also the teachers. Skinny was pleased that he had been able to talk with such authority about carnivals before the program began. It gave him the courage to take more of a part in the regular Sunday-school activities than usual.

During sentence prayers each pupil said a short prayer. A girl wearing a checkered pinafore asked that a sick playmate soon be well, and one in a pink ruffled dress asked that the Lord bless her best friend, who had gone all the way to Chattanooga just to spend three days. Lard's request was for good weather during the coming week. Skinny, who was next, knew this was on account of the carnival and said, "I hope you heard Lard, Lord. He's got a good idea." He realized at once that his prayer had seemed a bit more friendly, and maybe less solemn, than some of the others. More slowly, and in a low tone, he added, "If it be Thy will, maybe a sprinkling of rain late at night would come in handy." He said "Amen" then and felt better that he had taken into consideration Miss Bessie's concern about dust, and had not sided altogether with Lard in promoting a dry spell.

At the end of the prayers the teacher told them that each one had asked for something. "Let's try again," she said, "and this time, why don't we all be thankful for something instead of making requests?"

They started again, and Skinny noticed that everybody seemed still to be concerned with whatever had been on his mind the first time. The girl who had a sick playmate was thankful that her friend was showing some improvement, and the one in the pink dress was thankful that she knew somebody who could go all the way to Chattanooga just to spend three days. And Lard thanked God in advance for the sunshine he felt was certainly due in the week to come.

Skinny was the only one to bring up a new subject. He said, "Thank You for everybody in this room." And would have said, "Bless each one," but that would have been asking for something. So he finished with, "And thank You for everybody not in this room too."

Next the group sang two songs and then separated for classes. Skinny went with the boys of his age, and the first thing the teacher did was to ask each one to say a verse of Scripture. "If you can't say one from memory, you may read from the Bible," she said.

Most of the boys said short, easy verses, after telling first where they were to be found. When Skinny's turn came he stood up and announced, "Proverbs twenty-one, verse nine," and then quoted: " 'It is better to dwell in a corner of the housetop, than with a brawling woman in a wide house.' "

Elmer asked, "Is that in the Bible?" and Lard said, "Say it again."

The teacher asked, "Couldn't you quote another verse?"

"Sure," said Skinny proudly and got to his feet once more. "Proverbs twenty-one, verse nineteen: 'It is better to dwell in the wilderness, than with a contentious and an angry woman.' "

"I didn't mean another one on that order," said the teacher. "Where did you learn those particular ones?"

"Roman taught 'em to me," explained Skinny. "He's an ex-convict who was in a chain gang on account of he got into a fight with his wife." The teacher didn't seem very glad to hear about this, but the boys looked so interested that Skinny continued. "He didn't really mean any harm, though. Else Miss Bessie couldn't have bailed him out."

The teacher said maybe they had better get back to the study of the Bible and called for more verses

When the other boys had run dry, Skinny had not quoted all that he knew by heart. He had got into ones Miss Bessie had helped him learn, which the teacher thought were more appropriate. Since he had outlasted the other boys in memory work, the teacher said he could now take the Bible and read one of his favorite passages to the class.

"One of my favorite passages?" asked Skinny, sounding alarmed.

"Just a few verses you especially like."

Skinny hesitated. "Can I just say 'em?" he asked.

"If you wish."

He rose slowly and looked around at his audience. "Maybe I'd better read," he said and reached for the Bible. He opened it to about the halfway mark and began quoting from memory but pretending to read.

"There be four things which are little upon the earth, but they are exceeding wise."

He turned the page as if he had run out of words on that one and looked toward the top of the next one and continued.

"The ants are a people not strong, yet they prepare their meat in the summer;

The conies are but a feeble folk, yet make they their houses in the rocks;

The locusts have no king, yet go they forth all of them by bands;

The spider taketh hold with her hands, and is in kings'
   palaces."

He closed the Bible, saying, "That's one of my
favorite passages."

The teacher said it was one of her favorites too, and
the class spent the rest of the period discussing the
verses from it. They were especially interested to learn
that conies are a kind of rabbit.

On the way home Skinny worried about whether it
had been wrong for him to make believe he was reading. It had never troubled his conscience to pretend to
read a newspaper, but the Bible was different.

Before he could worry more a truck came past,
headed toward the carnival grounds. Canvas covered
its bulging sides and top. He walked ahead and was
speculating as to what might have been under the
canvas, when another truck came along. He recognized
Ferris wheel seats and framework piled high on it, just
as somebody called, "HEY, SKINNY!"

It was Calvin, sitting on a pillow strapped to the
right front fender, hanging on to a headlight with one
hand and waving with the other.

6 ↑↑↑↑↑↑↑ *Plans*

On Sunday afternoons Daddy Rabbit customarily took Miss Bessie and Skinny for drives. The day the carnival arrived Skinny suggested that maybe Calvin would like to come too.

Daddy Rabbit said, "I'm sure he's needed to help set up the Ferris wheel. But I'll take you and him on an outing before he leaves."

Skinny was sorry that Calvin could not join them that same afternoon, but cheered up when Daddy Rabbit invited him to steer the automobile.

Miss Bessie asked, "Are you sure he's big enough?"

"Of course he is," said Daddy Rabbit, turning onto a side road. He stopped the car, and Skinny moved up front and sat in the middle. Daddy Rabbit started the car again and gradually let Skinny take over. All the while Miss Bessie said such things as, "Now be careful! Both of you, be careful!"

Daddy Rabbit did not put his hands on the steering wheel for more than a mile, and Skinny was just saying, "Why, this is plumb easy," when a chipmunk ran onto the road. Skinny turned the wheel sharply to the left, and the car swerved. Then he turned it too far to the right. Daddy Rabbit put on the brakes and took over the steering—too late to keep the right front wheel out of the ditch.

When Daddy Rabbit had succeeded in backing the car onto the road again, he directed Skinny to take over. "Reckon I better?" asked Skinny nervously.

"Sure," said Daddy Rabbit, "I have confidence in you." And Skinny steered all the way back to the hotel.

After supper he asked permission to walk out to see how things were going at the carnival, but Miss Bessie thought he had better not. "It won't open till tomorrow," she said, "and there'll be plenty of time during the week for you to go."

On Monday morning he mopped the kitchen and dining room as soon as the breakfast dishes were put away. Then he ran to the store to fetch a bottle of vanilla flavoring Peachy had left off her main order. Next he shucked corn and set the tables for lunch. He would be ahead of his schedule by afternoon and could maybe look up Calvin. Everybody was always suggesting that he find boys his own age and play for a while.

After lunch he cleared the dining room of dirty dishes in record time and got set to ask if he could visit the carnival. But Miss Bessie came into the kitchen then with what she considered good news. She had purchased three bushels of butter beans from a produce peddler at a bargain price. She said, "Peachy, if you'll wash a batch of jars and get down the big pressure cooker, the rest of us will sit out on the back porch and do the shelling. If we work fast, we'll have them canned by night."

Skinny pretended to be glad. A sight of money would be saved on the winter grocery bill. But he mentioned later that he might walk out to the carnival that night, if Miss Bessie didn't have any objection.

She didn't mind at all and in the evening, before he left, gave him money to spend. She was even more generous than she had been the week tent movies were running. With the coins jingling in a Bull Durham tobacco sack stuffed into his pocket, Skinny hurried toward the carnival.

Before he was there he saw the lights of the amusements. Nearer, he heard the sounds of them. There was the music of the merry-go-round, mixed with trumpet notes from one side show and drum rolls from another. Above everything, he heard the barkers. The loudest one kept repeating, "How can you lose? Oh, how can you lose?"

Calvin was not at the Ferris wheel. His mother was in the ticket booth and his father was running the wheel, but they were busy. Skinny didn't want to disturb them and decided to walk around and come back later.

The first place he visited was a fishing game. The man who ran it was the one who chanted, "How can you lose? Oh, how can you lose?" A trough of water ran along the front of the concession with fish-shaped pieces of wood floating on top. Ten cents entitled a customer to dip out a "fish." The number on the bottom of it would be the number of the prize won.

The prizes were lined up on a stair-step rack and each of them appeared to Skinny to be worth much more than a dime. Wondering how the man could be so generous, he stepped up to try his luck. If he waited till later the place would be fished out—it being such a bargain.

He paid for a turn and with the dipper pulled out a wooden fish. He handed it to the man and waited to see whether he had won himself a blanket or a clock or a wrist watch or maybe just a horse statue.

"Number eighty-two," said the man and reached

back of him to a marker with the same number. The prize there was a balloon with a noisemaker on the end of it.

Skinny said, "Well, I'll declare. I didn't even see that one, it was so little."

"Only little prize here," announced the man. "Your luck's bound to improve."

"Yes," said Skinny, taking another dime from the Bull Durham sack, "it ought to do that." All the while he kept an eye on "number eighty-two," which the man had put back in the water. He didn't want to catch it again.

On his second try he fished out number fifty-eight. "You've won a genuine celluloid bird-caller," said the man. He handed over a whistle of the sort Skinny knew for a fact sold at two for a nickel in the drugstore.

"Try again," said the man. "The good ones are still in the pond." Skinny was examining his prizes. "Five cents a turn from here on," continued the man. "Reduced rate for good customers."

Skinny tried the whistle and it didn't work. He looked toward the sky and then back at the man. "Big fish won't bite on a night like this," he said.

"Why not?"

"The moon ain't right," said Skinny and laughed heartily as he walked away. He hoped he could remember to tell Roman about thinking up such a joke all by himself.

He went around to the Ferris wheel again and Calvin was still not there. A woman close by advertised, "Let a gypsy tell your fortune," and he went across to where she sat. When he learned that she charged a dollar a fortune he started away. She called out that she also answered questions. "Two for a quarter," she said. "And I can see into the future."

Skinny paid for two questions and followed her into the tent. He asked first if he was likely to be skinny for the rest of his life. "I wouldn't mind if your magic says I'm gonna fleshen up a bit."

"It's not magic," said the woman, gazing into a big glass ball. Then she said, half under her breath, "Skinny, skinny, always skinny." She wiped off one side of the ball to get a better look and continued in a low voice, speaking very slowly. "Bones . . . skin and bones . . . nothing but skin and bones."

Suddenly she said, "No!" so loudly that Skinny jumped. "It's not you." She was talking faster now. "It was somebody else. But now I see you. There you are over there." She leaned from side to side, looking into the future from different angles. "I didn't recognize you," she explained, "because you had put on so much weight."

Skinny smiled warmly as she asked him, "What's your other question?"

"The next one's my real problem," he said. "Where do you think I'll live from now on?"

"At home," answered the woman, not even looking down.

"I don't have a regular home. Couldn't you maybe peek into that contraption and—"

The gypsy interrupted him. "It's not a contraption, it's a crystal ball," and before Skinny could say that that was what he meant, she was hovering over it. "Houses!" She moaned. "Little houses . . . tumble-down houses . . . haunted houses . . ." She squinted her eyes. "I see one clearer now. It has a crumbling brick chimney."

"Is the front porch sort of caving in?"

"Yes," said the woman excitedly. "The front porch needs repair."

"That's where I *used* to live," said Skinny. "I want to know about the future one."

"Fear not," said the gypsy. "I can see another house now, a big one painted white." She waved her hands and leaned way back.

Skinny stood up. "Let me see," he said. "I'll tell you if it's the hotel." He looked down and saw nothing except the glass ball.

"You've broken the spell," said the gypsy, "but you've had your money's worth anyhow." And she led the way outside.

Skinny went back to the Ferris wheel and this time found his friend. "I've been waiting for you," said Calvin.

"I was by here two or three times."

"I took a nap while I was waiting," said Calvin, motioning toward a tent, "on account of I stayed up last night helping put the wheel together." Then he lowered his voice, "But it's the last time I'll have to do that. We're running away."

"Who is?"

"Me and you," said Calvin. "We agreed on it last time, don't you remember?"

"We just talked about it."

"Look, won't you have to go to an orphans' home?"

"In a few weeks," said Skinny. "But I've heard tell it's not so bad."

"Not so bad!" exclaimed Calvin. "Why, they'll have somebody looking after you all the time. It'll be as bad as having a mother and father of your own."

"They'll see that I get some schooling," said Skinny, "and that's what I need. Why, I ain't even got enough learning to play that Bingo game here at the carnival."

"It's easy."

"I watched it for a while but never did get the whole hang of it."

"Look," said Calvin, "I'll teach you to read and write. And now that we've settled that, ain't you glad we're running away?"

"Where'll we go?"

"Fort Valley. I got it figured out."

Calvin's mother called to ask him to run across to the freak show and get a five-dollar bill changed for her. He was gone a minute and continued with his plan when he came back. "The freight train that passes through here after midnight goes all the way to Fort Valley. I heard somebody saying so."

Skinny wanted to know what they would do there, and Calvin said that they could get a job packing peaches. "And we'll sleep under the packing sheds at night and use our wages to buy food. If peach season is over, we'll do something else. You can always get a job if you're sixteen."

Skinny's mouth dropped open. "We ain't near that old!"

"We'll pretend we are," said Calvin. "We'll comb our hair out of our eyes and stand up straight." Smiling proudly, he added, "That ought to fool 'em."

In bed that night, Skinny couldn't go to sleep for thinking. He thought about the hotel and how nice it would be to stay there permanently. But if he was going to an orphanage, and it looked as if he would be sent to that one at the edge of the mountains before long, then maybe running off was the thing to do. That way he could work for a living and not be a bother to anybody. And maybe he and Calvin would have themselves some good times.

Just then R. F. D., napping on a rag rug in a corner

of the room, whimpered. "What's the matter, pup?" asked Skinny softly. "Did you have a bad dream?"

R. F. D. padded across to the side of the bed. "If I went to the orphanage," whispered Skinny, "I'd have to leave you behind." He reached down and patted the dog. "But if I ran off, I could take you with me." R. F. D. hopped onto the bed and nuzzled close until they both went to sleep.

The next afternoon Skinny went to the carnival early after lunch. Calvin was unfolding canvas covers for the Ferris wheel seats. "It may rain," he said, looking up at the dark sky. In a lower tone he asked, "Did you decide?"

"Yes," answered Skinny, "I guess so."

"Are you going with me?"

"Yes, I guess so," repeated Skinny, not sounding as interested as Calvin, who went on to say that they would leave that very night.

"Let's wait till the end of the week," suggested Skinny. "It's a pity to go while there's a carnival in town."

"No," said Calvin. "Tonight's the time." He said they could meet at the freight platform of the depot at midnight, and when the train stopped they would climb into a boxcar and be off to Fort Valley.

Skinny hoped the idea made sense. It had seemed all right during the morning, before the weather turned off cloudy.

"Come on," said Calvin, "I'll get us a free turn on the swings." And he led the way to the only ride he liked.

Afterward Skinny bought them each a candy apple. He mentioned as they ate that he was concerned about Miss Bessie. It was a shame to cause her any grief. "Maybe I ought to tell her that we're leaving. She'd understand."

"You're crazy," said Calvin. "Write her a card and we can mail it as soon as we get there. It will come back on the same train we go down on. You won't hardly be missed before then."

Skinny frowned, and Calvin laughed. "I keep forgetting you can't write," he said. "Well, I'll write the card for you."

Skinny felt a little easier then, and before long the sun came out and everything seemed better. The music from the merry-go-round was livelier, the candy apple tasted sweeter, and even the voices of the barkers took on a cheery note. He heard above all the rest: "How CAN YOU LOSE? OH, HOW CAN YOU LOSE?"

7 ’’’’’’’ *The Freight Platform
at Midnight*

Skinny was not in a hurry to finish clearing the dishes
from the dining room. He kept thinking about this
being his last time. Peachy told him, "It'd be con-

siderate of you to move a little faster. You knows this is my Prayer Meeting night."

Roman spoke up. "I ain't never seen the beat. Whenever one of you is in a rush, the other one's in a slow-moving notion. Why can't you be like me and have a regular pace?"

Peachy sniffed. "Because your regular pace is so slow we'd turn into snails. I done give up on you, but Skinny can step about when the spirit moves him."

Skinny thanked her for the compliment and hurried along to finish his part of the work. He wanted to be remembered at the hotel for being of a cooperative nature.

Peachy left as soon as the kitchen was clean, and Roman and Skinny sat on the grass in the back yard to cool off. R. F. D. chased back and forth between them. After a while Roman decided to mosey across town to Peachy's church. "Prayer Meeting ought to be breaking up before long," he said, "and some gal might need me to walk home with her."

"I thought you got in so much trouble with your wife that you stayed away from gals," said Skinny. He hoped Roman would reconsider and sit back down. It usually didn't bother him to be alone, but he had a worrying mind tonight, and the thought of sitting in the night air by himself was not tempting. And if he went to his room he might go to sleep and not wake up in time to meet Calvin.

Roman jogged up and down on one foot that had gone to sleep. Skinny continued, "You said your brawling wife cured you from further interest in womankind." In an almost pleading tone he added, "Them was your exact words."

Roman laughed. "I reckon the cure warn't permanent," he said and walked toward the sidewalk.

Skinny stayed on in the yard. Enough light came from the kitchen windows for him to throw a stick across the grass and let R. F. D. fetch it. The stick was being retrieved for the third time when Miss Bessie called him. She and Daddy Rabbit were going for a ride. Would he care to come along?"

Ordinarily he would have shot around to the road and been sitting in the car before Miss Bessie and Daddy Rabbit got there. This time he walked through the hotel and was so long in reaching the front of it that he and R. F. D. almost got left.

He had stopped in the back hall and tried on his white coat. He considered wearing it to Fort Valley but changed his mind. Miss Bessie might hire a town boy after he was gone, and the coat could be a uniform again. Besides, it was too dressed-up for packing peaches.

During the ride Daddy Rabbit told stories about his construction jobs, but Skinny did not show his usual interest in hearing them. One was about the time Daddy Rabbit had fallen off a bridge during a flash flood. "It came close to being the end of me," he said, and Skinny didn't even ask what happened next.

After the ride Skinny said, "Good-night," and started to the back porch. After a few steps he stopped and turned around.

"Is something wrong?" asked Miss Bessie.

"No, ma'am," Skinny said awkwardly. "I just want to tell both of you . . . that is, I mean . . ." At last he blurted out, "Thank you for the kind deeds."

"Why, you're welcome," she answered. "And I appreciate what you do for me."

"What's got into everybody?" said Daddy Rabbit. "What's all this talk?"

"Nothing," Skinny said. "I'm just feeling . . ." He hesitated, looking down at his feet. "I'm just feeling thankful for kind deeds," he concluded and hurried away.

By the time the town clock struck eleven-thirty, it seemed to Skinny that he had been awake half the night. He went to his room and got the cold biscuits, the bag of them he had saved from supper in case he or Calvin or R. F. D. cared for nourishment before morning. Then he felt in his pocket to make certain the card he had bought at the post office was still there, along with a pencil stub. Calvin would write the card first thing in the morning, and they would mail it to Miss Bessie. It would keep her from worrying about him.

With R. F. D. close at his heels he started to the depot. Not once did he look back at the hotel. A final view of it might stick in his mind too long. Besides, it was too dark a night to see clearly. Even the people he met along the way were blurry outlines. The only person he recognized was one of the older boys he had seen around town. They met under the street light across from the filling station and the boy said, "If you're headed to the carnival, it's about shut up for the night." He didn't turn back to see if any attention was paid to his comment, and Skinny was glad. It saved him from having to make up a reason for being out walking at such a late hour.

At the depot Skinny went past the ticket office, which was locked up tight, and around to the freight ramp on the far side of the building. It was dark there, and he called, "Are you here, Calvin?" No answer came.

He almost stumbled over two crates near the edge of the platform and was about to sit down on one of them when a car came along the road out front. The light from it put him in full view, but the driver did not look in his direction. Skinny moved farther back, finding a safer place behind the big scales that were always on the platform.

By the time the town clock struck twelve Calvin still had not shown up. Skinny wondered what was keeping him. Then came the sound of footsteps. He waited a minute and was set to call, "Here I am," when a match was struck and he saw that it was not Calvin. Instead, a large, red-faced man was there. He lit a lantern with the match and adjusted the wick. Next he began to push the two crates from the platform onto a cart. Afterward he rolled the cart out alongside the tracks and sat down on one end of it and waited. The night grew still again.

Skinny kept a sharp ear out for more footsteps. He hoped Calvin would not make a lot of noise or they would be caught before they had a chance to sneak onto the train. He was worrying about this when all of a sudden there was a loud whistle. After that a humming noise came from the rails and the whistle sounded again, louder than before. The headlight of the engine came into view as the locomotive rounded a curve. A minute later the train was clanging to a halt at the station, and the red-faced man pushed his cart up to one of the boxcars. He slid the door open and shoved the cargo inside. A freight handler aboard the next car called that there was nothing to be unloaded, and the red-faced man waved his lantern. He pushed his cart under the ramp as the train pulled out, and was opening the light to blow out the flame when R. F. D. barked.

"Who's there?" called the man and brought his lantern nearer. R. F. D. ran across the platform and was asked in a gentle tone, "What are you doing here, puppy-dog?" R. F. D. barked again, and the man continued, "You better get along home before morning or somebody will be worried." He blew out his lantern, and Skinny waited until his footsteps were in the distance before stirring.

"Come on, let's go," he called. R. F. D. didn't come at once and was scolded. "All right, I'll leave you here. I'm put out with you anyway for almost getting us in trouble." He started from the ramp. "And I'm put out with Calvin too." R. F. D. trotted after him.

Skinny was always sorry when things didn't go according to plan. What was the use in making arrangements if you weren't going to act according to them? But halfway home he decided this was one time it might be best that plans had not worked out. He hurried to the hotel and slipped back into his room, hoping nobody would know that he had almost chased off to Fort Valley.

The next day he was in what Peachy called an "off-and-on" mood. For a while he sang as he went about his morning chores. Then he became long-faced and did not even smile while the funny papers were being read.

He cheered up again as he ran the carpet sweeper over the parlor rug. It was good to be back at the hotel, working with people he liked. Next, a gloomy spell set in. Calvin ought not to have let him down like that.

Why couldn't he have at least come to the depot and said that the plan was off, instead of leaving him and R. F. D. huddled behind those scales until the train had come and gone?

He had a notion to go right now and tell Calvin so. On second thought maybe it would be smarter of him to say it hadn't mattered one way or the other. He might even make out like he hadn't gone to the depot either. He would say he knew all the time it had been a joke.

Peachy came in and asked if he had seen Roman. She wanted him to wring the necks of five frying chickens.

Skinny immediately felt good again. He had been so wrapped up in himself he had forgotten that this was Wednesday. And right off he couldn't think of anything finer than chicken night at Miss Bessie's hotel.

There were more guests than usual for supper, and it looked for a while as if they were going to eat everything Peachy had prepared. Skinny brought out the last platter of fried chicken and announced as he served it, "There's home-churned ice cream for dessert, folks. Save room for ice cream."

As it turned out there were a few pieces of chicken left, but even Peachy admitted that she and Skinny and Roman could have done with more. She guessed it would take six fryers from now on.

During the clearing up afterward, Peachy asked if anybody knew the particulars about last night's accident at the carnival.

"I heard something about it across town," said Roman, and Skinny asked, "What accident?"

"On the swings," said Peachy. "One of the seats fell out while it was moving, and somebody got broken up."

Roman said, "Nobody from around here, though. It was one of the carnival crowd."

Skinny stood still, a dazed expression on his face. Then he put his tray on the kitchen table. "I've finished bringing in the dishes," he said and hurried from the room.

He was out of breath when he reached the carnival but did not slow down until he was at the Ferris wheel. He was about to ask the woman at the ticket booth if her son had been in the accident when he saw Calvin standing nearby. He walked over to him and said, "You ain't bandaged up none."

"Why should I be bandaged up?"

"I thought you fell off the swings last night."

Calvin shrugged. "That was little Grover. Served him right for not hanging on."

"I heard he was hurt something awful."

"Just broke his collar bone," said Calvin, tapping his own shoulder to indicate the location of the break. "He's still able to help his pa at the whip."

Skinny asked, "Is that why you didn't show up last night?"

"No, I just decided I didn't want to run away."

"Why didn't you come tell me? I was waiting and waiting."

"Figured you'd know," said Calvin. His mother called to ask him to buy a cup of coffee for her, and he and Skinny walked across to the tent café. Calvin said, "But I've changed my mind again. We'll run off tonight. You be there the same as before."

"No," said Skinny. "I've decided it's not the thing to do."

"All right," said Calvin, "I'll go by myself. Wait and see."

"I'll wait," said Skinny and started away. He turned back and added, "But if you're still here, I might see you tomorrow night."

"We can run away then."

"That ain't what I mean," said Skinny. "I'll come back and we can fool around the carnival."

"Who cares about a carnival?" said Calvin and headed toward the Ferris wheel.

Skinny's spirits were not high as he walked home, but he was pleased when he arrived at the hotel to find Miss Bessie and Daddy Rabbit back from their ride.

"Want to hear some nice news?" called Miss Bessie.

"Yes, ma'am," said Skinny, entering the parlor. "That would do me a sight of good."

"Well," said Miss Bessie, lowering her voice, "you're not to tell a soul, but Mr. Rabbit and I are going to be married."

"Well, I'll declare!" said Skinny. "That sure is nice."

Daddy Rabbit was smiling, and Miss Bessie looked happy too.

Then Skinny remembered that Miss Bessie had said she wouldn't let him go off to an orphans' home if she were a married woman. He grinned enthusiastically and said, "This is a happy occasion, ain't it?"

8 ⁊⁊⁊⁊⁊⁊⁊⁊ *Calvin's Visit*

Skinny straddled the biggest limb of the maple tree. "All right," he said, "I'm ready," and Daddy Rabbit tossed him the rope.

They were making a back-yard swing from an old automobile tire, one Daddy Rabbit no longer needed. It had been Skinny's idea to hang it from the sweet gum in the front yard. That way, if the porch ever got crowded, a guest could just step into the yard and swing in the tire for a while. Miss Bessie hadn't taken to the idea, nor to the one for whitewashing the tire and laying it in a flower bed, planted with whatever she liked best. Daddy Rabbit did not appear interested at the time, but the following Saturday noon he came in with a plowline. "It's for your own private swing," he told Skinny, and immediately after lunch they set about hanging the tire from the maple.

"Tie the rope the other way," called Daddy Rabbit, holding his straw hat to shade his eyes. "No, cross it over on this side before you loop it." He was giving instructions from the ground. "That-a-boy! Now pull the end through the opening."

After the knot was securely tied, Skinny leaned over from the limb to come down by way of the rope. "Careful," called Daddy Rabbit, "or you'll burn your hands."

"Oh, I know how to slide," said Skinny. "In the old days I used a rope to get down from our barn loft." He wrapped one leg around the rope, pressed against it with his other foot to keep from sliding too fast, and slid to the ground.

He sat in the tire and gave a push. Deciding immediately that it was hung at the right height, he suggested that Daddy Rabbit try it.

"No," said Daddy Rabbit, "I've got to go across town." He flicked a speck of dust from his polka-dot hatband.

Skinny said he believed he would just swing until Calvin came.

"I'd forgotten this was the day he's paying you a visit," said Daddy Rabbit, starting from the yard. "I'll be back before long and take you and him out to the new bridge."

Skinny called after him, "That's a ripsnorting idea. We'll be waiting." He gave a shove with his foot to make the swing go higher. Talking to R. F. D., who sat near the tree trunk, he said, "Me and you sure are lucky to have Daddy Rabbit." R. F. D. lifted his head as if he understood every word. "We're lucky to have Miss Bessie too. It was her idea to invite Calvin over."

Just then the doorbell rang. Instead of going through the hotel Skinny ran around it. He hid behind a crape myrtle bush at the end of the porch and asked in a deep voice, "What d'you want?"

"I see you," said Calvin, and Skinny came out from his hiding place. Both boys laughed.

"If you'll wait here," said Skinny, "I'll show you how I usually answer the door." He went into the hotel, calling back, "Ring the bell again in about a minute."

When the bell rang, Skinny walked up the hall in his white coat. "Howdy!" he said, as if greeting a new-comer. "Welcome to this-here hotel." He stepped out onto the porch. "What can I do for you, sir?"

"I'd like to rent a room or two," said Calvin, affecting a businesslike tone.

"I see," said Skinny. "And could I ask what line of work you're in?"

"I'm a gangster," answered Calvin, and they both were laughing when Miss Bessie came onto the porch.

"Wouldn't you boys like a glass of milk and some cake?" she asked.

"That's a kind thought," said Skinny and led the way to the kitchen, where Peachy had left a caramel cake on the table. They ate two thick slices each, drank iced tea instead of milk, and went into the back yard to play.

They stopped first at the tire swing, and while Calvin had a turn in it Skinny propped himself against the tree. "Daddy Rabbit's coming back after a while," he said, "and take you and me out to the bridge that's being built. We'll get to poke around the machinery, on account of him being with us."

"Want to play catch while we wait?" asked Calvin, reaching into his back pocket. "I borrowed a ball from the throwing concession."

After pitching the ball back and forth to each other for a long time, they sat down in the shade to rest. Skinny said he expected Daddy Rabbit would be back any minute now. "It was smart of you to bring along a ball," he added. "Do you have borrowing privileges all over the carnival?"

"Not all," answered Calvin.

"What if you had brought a rifle from the shooting gallery? We could have set up a tin can and had ourselves a target practice."

"The gallery man ain't sporty about such as that," said Calvin. "But the Bingo operator lent me a prize just for today." He held up a jackknife. "We could have target practice with this."

"I don't expect we'd have time to get started," said Skinny, "since Daddy Rabbit will come for us before long." He looked toward the woodpile. "But while we're waiting, the back of that shed would make a fine target."

They walked over to have a look at it, and Calvin took a sunflower leaf and stuck the stem of it between two of the boards. Next he stepped back to what he considered a proper distance and drew a line. "Stand here," he said, "and see if you can hit the leaf."

Skinny took the knife and threw it, missing the leaf by several feet.

"You hit the wall anyway," said Calvin, pulling the knife from the board. He backed up to the line, took careful aim, and hurled the knife. It pinned the leaf against the woodshed. "I'm good at it," he announced, as if Skinny couldn't tell. "My uncle used to be the knife-thrower at the carnival."

He told Skinny to try again, showing him how to take better aim. Skinny didn't hit the leaf that time either but he came closer to it than before. His aim improved with each try, although he never managed to do as well as Calvin.

The town clock struck four, and Skinny said, "Goodness, I didn't know it was that late. We'd better gather the eggs." He ran into the hotel to get a basket. "Daddy Rabbit is still off somewhere," he said on his return. "I wonder what's holding him up."

In the henhouse, Calvin helped collect the eggs, after being advised to handle them carefully. "Could you get a chicken to lay an egg for us now?" he asked.

"That ain't the way hens operate."

"Then how do they operate?"

"They have to be in the right notion," said Skinny as they walked toward the hotel. He told Calvin to wait for him at the tire swing while he carried the eggs inside. When he returned he explained more about egg-laying. "Usually it's in the morning," he said, "and the hens sit on the nest for a long time. Then all of sudden they hop off cackling, carrying on because they've laid an egg."

"I think I'll be a farmer when I grow up," said Calvin.

"I'm torn between that and running a hotel," said Skinny. An automobile was heard out front, and he stopped to listen. "That ain't him," he said when the car drove on.

Roman came across the yard, and Skinny asked if he

wouldn't tell Calvin some of his interesting chain-gang experiences. Roman laughed. "They warn't all that interesting," he said. "And besides, I've got to bring up the cows."

"Cows," said Calvin, hopping up from the swing. "You got cows here?"

"Three," said Skinny, motioning toward the end of the yard, where pecan trees screened the view of the barn.

"Usually they come up at milking time," said Roman, "but lately the grazing has been so good across the branch that I have to go for them."

"We'll get 'em for you," said Skinny. "And if you see Daddy Rabbit, tell him we'll be right back."

Two of the cows were eating grass when Skinny and Calvin found them, and the other one was resting under a tree. "I like this better than anything we've done," said Calvin. "Could you get them to give milk while I watch? Or do they have to be in the right notion too?"

"Roman does the milking," said Skinny, jumping over a blackberry bush to head off one of the cows. "But he won't mind if you watch."

At the barn the red calf rushed from a stable to meet its mother. Skinny ran in and pushed him out of the barn and shut the door.

"How come you to do that?" asked Calvin.

"He'd get all the milk if he had the chance,"

said Skinny. He rubbed the calf, which appeared more interested in getting back to its mother than in being petted.

Roman came along with two empty pails, and Calvin followed him into the barn. Skinny walked up to the hotel and returned in a few minutes with the report that he had not seen Daddy Rabbit. Calvin was having a milking lesson by then, which he said was better than going for a ride anyway.

When the milking was finished and the calf had been turned in with its mother, Calvin decided it was about time for him to start home. They went into the hotel, and Miss Bessie said, "I was hoping you would have supper with us."

"Me too," said Calvin. "When will it be ready?"

"Not until later."

"I'll get whipped if I don't get home by dark."

"We'd hate for that to happen," said Miss Bessie, turning to Skinny. "Show him around the hotel while Peachy and I make some sandwiches."

Calvin seemed interested in the sights that were pointed out to him. "Let's ramble through those belongings," he suggested as they passed one of the rented rooms. There were a watch chain and penknife on top of the dresser. "We might come across something interesting."

"No," said Skinny firmly. "It ain't right to meddle." He led the way to the stairs, and they discussed whether they were too big to slide down the banister rail. Before they decided one way or the other, Miss Bessie called them to come for their refreshments.

They ate ham and tomato sandwiches, bananas, and cake, and drank all the milk they wanted. Peachy was at the breadboard kneading dough. "The skinnier they are, the more they eats," she said, and the boys laughed, helping themselves to one more slice of caramel cake.

Calvin asked Miss Bessie as he was leaving, "Would you keep me in mind if you ever need another boy to come live here?"

Miss Bessie smiled. "You must visit us again," she said. "But your parents wouldn't like it if you came to stay."

"Oh, they wouldn't care," said Calvin. "And even if they did, I'd just run away." He poked Skinny, and both of them laughed.

In the dining room before supper, Skinny filled the saltcellars and pepper shakers. He thanked Miss Bessie for giving him and Calvin a good time.

"This hotel is your home," she said, arranging a bouquet of four-o'clocks at the sideboard. "After Mr. Rabbit and I are married, we plan to adopt you officially. In the meantime—well, you belong here as much as anybody, and it's only fitting for you to have friends visit you."

"I don't know if I can think up anybody else to

invite," said Skinny. "But thank you, anyway." Then he asked, "What became of Daddy Rabbit? Reckon I ought to hunt around and see if I can locate him?"

"No," answered Miss Bessie, "we mustn't try to keep track of him." She concluded, almost as if she were talking to herself, "He's been carefree so long, I don't know how he will take to settling down."

Skinny noticed a worried tone in her voice and told her, "He's gonna take to it just fine. You wait and see."

Miss Bessie smiled. "He's never stayed in one place more than a few months in his life. And he still loves moving around better than anything." She picked off a yellowed leaf from the four-o'clocks. "But I'm glad you're confident everything will be all right."

Suppertime came and Daddy Rabbit had still not returned to the hotel. "What if he took sick and had to be rushed off to a hospital somewhere?" said Skinny. "Or maybe he climbed out on the bridge and fell off and broke his bones all to pieces. Or he could have just dropped dead right by himself."

"Skinny!" scolded Miss Bessie. "How you talk!"

"I've heard of such things happening. I've heard of awful things."

"Well, you just stop having such thoughts. Mr. Rabbit will show up sooner or later."

In the parlor after the night work was finished, Skinny sensed that Miss Bessie was more worried than she pretended to be. He tried to cheer her with a long story about a man he and his pa had known who disappeared one time. "Everybody went around asking everybody else if they knew what had become of him," he said. "But nobody recollected seeing hair nor hide of him for close on to a month. Then one Saturday night he showed up at the general store and said he had been fishing. That was all the explanation he gave, and he bought syrup and fatback for the next week, same as always, and went home." Miss Bessie smiled, and Skinny concluded the story. "As far as I know, he ain't disappeared since."

Miss Bessie said, "I doubt if Mr. Rabbit has gone fishing."

"That's not what I meant," said Skinny. "I just meant that because he didn't show up for supper don't necessarily mean he's gone off and got in serious trouble or had an automobile wreck or maybe just keeled over dead from nothing at all."

"Bring the Bible," said Miss Bessie. "You must learn some new verses for Sunday school tomorrow."

Skinny fetched the Bible, and Miss Bessie turned to the Gospel according to Saint John. The part she read concerned the miracle of feeding a multitude of five thousand men with the lunch one boy had brought along.

Skinny practiced each verse afterward. That was his system. He would get one straight in his mind before moving to another. He quoted: " 'There is a lad here which hath five barley loaves, and two small fishes: but what are they among so many?' " When he came to the end of it he chuckled. "How many baskets of table scraps did you say were left over?"

Miss Bessie ran her finger down the page. "It says that they filled twelve baskets with the fragments of the five barley loaves after everyone had eaten."

"Ain't that something!" said Skinny. "I wish I'd been there to see ol' Philip and Simon Peter and all that crowd when Jesus up and stretched the lunch the way he did."

"It would have been interesting," agreed Miss Bessie, and Skinny declared, "It would have been a sight to behold!"

Someone in the doorway asked, "What would have been a sight to behold?" and they looked up to see Daddy Rabbit standing there.

9 '''''''' "This Hotel Ain't Meant to Be Lively"

"It'll be over in another week or two," said Skinny in an effort to console Peachy.

"Since Mr. Daddy Rabbit brought eleven more of his crowd to stay here," she muttered, "I don't get to take off my apron before it's time to put it on again."

"When the bridge is finished," said Skinny, "they'll all leave."

"Every last one of 'em," agreed Roman, who was chipping ice for supper.

Skinny couldn't say that not quite *every last one* would be leaving. He wished he could tell them that Daddy Rabbit would be staying, but it was a secret still. Even more he wished he could say, "And I won't be sent to the orphans' home—now that Miss Bessie's going to have a husband." He expected Roman and Peachy would be as happy about that as he was.

"I'll be glad when they all clear out," said Peachy, sighing as if the rush had lasted three years instead of only three weeks.

"Then you'll be complaining that things are too slow," said Roman. "There ain't no pleasing you, Peachy-gal. And besides, this hotel ain't never been so lively."

"This hotel ain't meant to be lively," muttered Peachy, opening the oven door to see if the biscuits had browned.

The rush at the hotel had been on since the Saturday Daddy Rabbit failed to get back in time to take Calvin and Skinny to see the new bridge. "I ran into some of the crowd from work," he had explained to Miss Bessie and Skinny that night, "and we rode up the highway. We got started talking about old times, and I just sort of forgot to come home." He had said more than once how sorry he was and then had told them interesting news. His friends who were rooming in Vickstown were not pleased with their hotel. And when he had bragged so much about Miss Bessie's, they all wanted to move there.

With the arrival of the new guests, a change had come over the hotel. There was extra work, of course—extra beds to be made, additional food to be prepared, more dishes to be put on the tables before meals and cleared away afterward. But there was also more excitement, furnished chiefly by the men themselves—more noise, more whistling and singing, more jokes and laughter than ever before.

Skinny suspected that even Peachy was enjoying the change. The night after she had complained about the work load, he noticed her standing in the kitchen doorway while supper was being served. She laughed along with everybody else at a story one of the men told. It was about a boarding house where all of them once lived. He said, "The lady who ran it never would believe that Daddy Rabbit was a construction worker. She thought he was a preacher."

"In another place," said Daddy Rabbit, "a café owner got it into her head that I was a district judge passing through town. I don't know why folks never believe I'm what I am."

One of the men said, "It's because you look too prosperous to be one of us." And another said, "Yeah, and you look too intelligent." They all laughed, and different ones came up with different reasons as to why

Daddy Rabbit's looks confused people. Skinny noticed that none of them said it was because Daddy Rabbit was older than the others. He started to say that he had figured out the genuine explanation but changed his mind. It came to him suddenly that the men knew the reason too, but just said funny things and pretended they didn't.

After supper Skinny sat on the back steps until he heard several cars drive away. Figuring almost everyone was out of the hotel, he got up and went inside. Maybe somebody had left a newspaper in the parlor.

Miss Bessie greeted him. "I wondered if you had gone to bed already."

Skinny said, "I thought I heard Daddy Rabbit's car drive off."

"You did, but he went without me." She reached over and patted R. F. D., who was sitting on the piano stool. "I don't know how it'll all work out."

"How what all will work out?"

"Mr. Rabbit and me. Sometimes I wonder." She looked toward the piano and gave a forced-sounding laugh. "I believe R. F. D. could play us a piece if he set his mind to it. Don't you?"

A frown came across Skinny's face. "Did Daddy Rabbit just drive off without you?" he asked.

This time Miss Bessie's laugh did not seem forced. "Why, no. He was meeting some of his friends at a barbecue place out on the highway, and I thought I'd better not stay out that late."

Skinny didn't think the barbecue place was all that far, and he hoped Miss Bessie wasn't tired of Daddy Rabbit. They ought to have gone on and got married when the notion struck them, that's what they ought to have done. If their plans fell through now—well, his chances of staying on at the hotel were as good as ended.

Or maybe, he thought, Daddy Rabbit was the one losing interest. He hoped not, but there was something he had noticed: Since so many of the bridge crew moved to the hotel, Daddy Rabbit spent a lot of his time chasing around with them.

He wished he could think of something cheerful to say to Miss Bessie but nothing appropriate came to him, so he asked if she had finished with the newspaper. "Me and Peachy and Roman might just glance at the funnies tomorrow if we can find the time."

Miss Bessie smiled as she handed him the paper. "You 'most always find the time, don't you?"

"Yes, ma'am," said Skinny. "But we don't slack off on our work to get to it."

Miss Bessie laughed. "I know you don't," she said, getting up to go to her room. She put her arm around Skinny's shoulder as she went past him. "And I'm glad you enjoy the funnies."

In the middle of the next week the construction workers reported that the bridge was nearly finished, and on Saturday afternoon they came in with the news that the job was done. They had received their next assignment and would leave early Sunday morning.

Miss Bessie decided to feed them a better supper than had been planned and sent Skinny to the market. "Ain't it splendid?" he asked R. F. D. on the way. "Fried chicken twice in one week!"

Later in the afternoon he was working on the scuppernong arbor in the side yard when Daddy Rabbit came out and offered to help. "Do you want me to push up that sagging two-by-four?" he asked, pointing to an overhead crossbar.

"Good idea," said Skinny, hurrying to prop a supporting piece underneath.

Next, they replaced a rotted corner post. After that, they reset one near the center that had fallen, and the repairs were all made. "It was easier than I thought," said Skinny, thanking Daddy Rabbit for the help. He reached overhead and pushed back leaves to expose large grapes. "In another week or two they'll be ripe," he continued. "Ain't you glad you'll be here instead of off with your crew? Your friends are liable to wind up next at some place that don't even have scuppernongs."

"That's the truth," said Daddy Rabbit perkily. He was silent a few seconds and looked out across the yard. "On the other hand," he continued thoughtfully, "there are different things at different places. And it's always fun to see what's next."

Skinny stopped admiring the crop of grapes. "I thought you were glad to be settling down?"

"Oh, I am," said Daddy Rabbit. "I don't wish for a minute that I could move out tomorrow when the others do."

"I remember what you said when you first got here," said Skinny, leaning on the post-hole digger.

"What was that?"

"You told me that moving around and meeting new folks all the time was jim-dandy. You said you wouldn't have your life any other way. Remember?"

"I might have thought that at the time."

"But we're gonna miss the rest of them, ain't we?" continued Skinny. "It won't be the same around here."

"We'll enjoy the peace and quiet," said Daddy Rabbit in not too convincing a tone. "If you don't need me, I think I'll go back inside."

The jokes during supper were mostly about Daddy Rabbit and how it wasn't going to seem right without him. He and Miss Bessie had not told their plans, and the men thought he was staying on at the hotel because he was tired of traveling around. They thought he wanted to get a job that would keep him in one place.

One of them said, "We must celebrate tonight if this is our last time together."

"I guess I'll just hang around the hotel," said Daddy Rabbit.

"We won't allow it," said one man, and the others agreed. Even Miss Bessie sided with them. "Have one last fling with your friends," she suggested, and after supper was over all the men left for the evening.

Miss Bessie offered to help Skinny with Bible verses when the work was finished, but he said he hadn't used up all the ones from last week. He suggested that they listen to the radio instead. The "Barn Dance" would be on.

R. F. D. came into the parlor when the program began and barked at the radio. That was his custom. He came into the room and barked whenever the radio was turned on, then lay down in front of it.

This time he barked, hopped onto a footstool, and sat there as if he had been anxious all week to hear some good fiddling. He left his seat only once during the program, when Uncle Ezra, one of the "Barn Dance" regulars, told a joke that made Skinny and Miss Bessie laugh more than usual. He ran to the radio, barked at it, and returned to his place.

"You're a sight!" said Skinny.

"He's funnier than the radio show," agreed Miss Bessie. And at bedtime she said, "I don't know how we could get along without R. F. D. He can be counted on to make us laugh."

In the morning the men were late getting downstairs

for breakfast. Skinny said he might ought to skip Sunday school and help them with their suitcases. Miss Bessie did not agree. The men could lift their own luggage if they chose to leave while he was not around.

After Sunday school he hurried back to the hotel. He might still be of help in loading the cars.

Miss Bessie was in the front yard when he got there. "The weeds are about to take my candytuft," she said. "Now that things have quieted down, I must pay more attention to the flowers."

"Did the men get off?" asked Skinny.

"Yes, they've all gone." She looked up and stared at him without speaking. Then she repeated softly, "They've *all* gone." The expression on her face told more than her voice.

"Not Daddy Rabbit?"

"Yes."

"Where's he gone?"

"With the others," answered Miss Bessie. "He was fit to be tied when the first carload pulled out. I could tell how much he wanted to be a part of the excitement—moving on, landing in a new place, seeing new sights."

Skinny asked, "Did you tell him to go?"

"I told him to suit himself."

"I don't believe he will stay gone," said Skinny.

Miss Bessie smiled. "He said he would come back, but I don't think we can count on it." She stepped into a flower bed. "He won't ever lose the urge to move on," she continued, "no matter how old he gets. Some folks are like that, and we shouldn't try to stop them—you or me or anybody else." Her voice quavered a tiny bit, and she concentrated on uncoiling a wiry runner from around one of her plants.

"That's a love-vine," said Skinny, looking at the weed that was choking a periwinkle.

10 ⟋⟋⟋⟋⟋⟋⟋ *Forty Miles Is a Far Piece*

For the next few days every time a car stopped out front Skinny would run to see who was there. By Wednesday he began to wonder if perhaps Miss Bessie had been right. Maybe Daddy Rabbit would not come back.

That evening in the parlor he said, "Well, it looks

like there ain't no getting around the orphans' home for me."

"I'm afraid not," said Miss Bessie.

Skinny pretended to be half concerned with finding the funnies in a newspaper that had been left there. "I was hoping maybe you would change your mind," he said. "I was hoping maybe you would keep me on."

Miss Bessie looked at him. "Put the paper down," she said softly, "and let's talk." He folded the paper as she continued, "I *do* want to keep you. More than anything, I want you to be here."

Skinny smiled, pushing himself back to a more comfortable position on the sofa. "Then I'll just stay," he said happily. "We settled that in a hurry, didn't we?"

"It's not that simple," said Miss Bessie. "I want to do what's best for you."

"This hotel is best for me, there ain't no doubt about that."

"I talked it over with the preacher," continued Miss Bessie, "since he's one of the ones making arrangements to get you in the church home. I asked if you couldn't stay on here."

"He don't mind, does he?"

"It's more a matter of what he thinks best for you. And, too, the county board has rules to go by."

Skinny could tell from her tone that it was all settled. "Couldn't you maybe talk to the board? They might not see the need to send me off."

"I went by there," said Miss Bessie, "and we discussed it for a long time. They insisted that I shouldn't keep you, even if they could allow it. I don't have a very firm hand, you know."

"Oh, I don't need a firm hand."

Miss Bessie smiled. "You'll be around a lot of children there. Why, you've been around nothing but adults all your life. You've hardly had a childhood."

"I've had all the childhood I need," said Skinny, his voice trembling just a little bit. "I don't see why I can't stay here. I could do a heap of jobs for you." He fidgeted with an armrest cover at the end of the sofa. "You'd be surprised at how hard I can work."

Miss Bessie came over and sat beside him. "You're not being sent away because you don't work hard; you must not think that at all." She put an arm around him. "And you're not being sent away because I don't want you here."

"Oh, I ain't never felt that you intentionally wanted to be rid of me."

Miss Bessie smiled. "I intentionally care so much for you that I'll give you up if it's for your own good. Can you understand that?"

"I'll try to," said Skinny, starting toward his room. Noticing how grieved Miss Bessie looked, he added, "I know it ain't your fault."

Thursday was a long day; there was time between chores for doing nothing. Skinny stood staring out a kitchen window in the afternoon. Peachy told him, "This place is plumb gloomy when you stands around with such a long face." There was no indication that she had been heard, and she spoke louder. "That orphans' home ain't but forty miles away."

Skinny turned to her and said, "Forty miles is a far piece." He would have looked out the window again, but she asked him to fetch apples from the back porch.

A few minutes later he was washing the apples in a big pan and handing them over to her. As she cored them for baking she talked. "They got lots of boys and girls where you're going," she said. "Won't that be nice?"

Skinny didn't answer, and Peachy continued, "I wishes you would take on a more hopeful outlook, child. You can be happy anywhere if you makes up your mind to it." She pointed toward herself and added, "It's what's inside you that counts. You has to be happy inside."

Roman, mopping the hall, called from the doorway, "Were you pointing toward your heart or your stomach?"

"We warn't talking to you," said Peachy.

"If you're trying to put Skinny in a better mood," Roman said, walking into the room, "I know something that'll perk him up."

Skinny asked, "What's that?" hoping there would

be a rumor that he could stay on at the hotel after all.

"I hear tell that the home you're going to runs one of the best farms in this end of the state," said Roman. "They're bound to let you work on it part of the time."

Peachy said, "Now won't that be dandy? You likes farming better than anything."

Skinny tried to think of something pleasant to say. He could tell they wanted to make him feel good. But nothing came to his mind so he bent his head and went back to washing apples.

On Friday morning Miss Bessie told him that he would be going to the orphans' home the next day. Knowing how it upset her to think of his leaving, he did not beg to stay. She wouldn't let him go if it weren't necessary. Instead he asked, "How will I get there?"

"They'll come for you. The preacher has made the plans."

"That takes care of everything except R. F. D.," said Skinny. "Once I decided I wouldn't go if he couldn't, but I reckon that wasn't smart. Do you suppose he could stay on here?"

"Of course," said Miss Bessie. "He will help keep up my spirits while you're away."

At that point R. F. D. came into the room. He turned his head at a funny angle and looked at each of them.

"Doesn't he feel important?" said Miss Bessie, and she and Skinny laughed. "Do you suppose he knows we're discussing his future?"

R. F. D. walked over to where Skinny was sitting and hopped into the chair beside him.

During the afternoon Miss Bessie asked Skinny to come with her to the dry-goods store. "We'll buy clothes for you," she said on the way.

"I still have the last ones you bought me," said Skinny, referring to most of the clothes he owned. When he had moved to town his personal belongings were so few that he had carried them in a paper bag. The clothes he had acquired since were gifts from Miss Bessie.

At the store she began to pick out light-weight pants for him.

"I got plenty of summer duds," said Skinny.

"You could use a few more," said Miss Bessie, selecting shirts, two pairs of pants, and new overalls. "Now we must buy a few winter things," she said, putting a cap on him to make certain it was the right size. Next she bought him wool pants, a lumber jacket, two pairs of shoes—one pair with high tops—and a suit. The suit was so fine that he doubted if even Daddy Rabbit owned anything as handsome.

"Ain't no use in buying so much," said Skinny,

pointing to the stack of clothes at one end of the counter. "It's more than I can tote." He was careful to hold on to the suit as he pointed, lest anyone think he wanted it returned.

"That reminds me," said Miss Bessie, turning to the man who was waiting on her. "What do you have in the way of luggage?" Before Skinny realized it, she had purchased a small trunk and asked that the clothes be put into it. "Send everything over to the hotel," she directed.

They walked home by way of the drugstore, stopping to eat store-bought ice cream and to buy a hairbrush. "I imagine they'll have a hairbrush at the orphanage," Skinny protested. "Ain't no use in me taking one."

Miss Bessie laughed. "You just don't want to have to use it," she said, paying for the purchase.

That night Skinny went into the parlor when the work was finished. He was wearing the white coat that he called his uniform. He took it off, and underneath was the jacket to his new suit. Miss Bessie laughed. "Are you warm enough?" she asked, fanning herself with a folded section of the *Atlanta Constitution*.

"I just wanted to see how it felt," he explained.

"It looks nice on you," said Miss Bessie. She looked at the white coat he had hung on a chair back. "We should clean that one for you."

"I don't think I'll take it along," said Skinny. "It's been my uniform here, but I don't guess I'll be needing it any more."

"Then I'll put it away for you till next summer," said Miss Bessie, and she told him that he would be allowed to spend his summers at the hotel. "I kept hounding the board about adopting you," she said, "and when they wouldn't consent, I got started on summer plans. They had to agree on them to get rid of me." She chuckled. "While they were yielding, I made them throw in Christmas too!"

She and Skinny both laughed, and Miss Bessie said, "Of course, you needn't come back if you don't want to. You might be so happy at—"

Skinny interrupted. "Oh, I'll come back. I promise not to ever be that happy."

And Saturday morning he looked as if he had promised not to ever be happy at all. He stood gazing out the kitchen window for a long time. Peachy said, "I done told you that place ain't but forty miles away." Before he could say, "Forty miles is a far piece," Peachy asked, "Couldn't you smile just a fraction?"

Skinny said slowly, "They're coming to get me today."

"Don't say it that way, child," said Peachy. "You make it sound like they're coming to fetch you in a hearse."

"They're coming to take me off," said Skinny,

"that's all I know." He went out of the kitchen before Peachy could talk about hopeful outlooks and being happy inside yourself.

At the woodpile Roman stopped working and asked, "Got your trunk packed?"

"It's packed," said Skinny, "but I could unpack it in a hurry if Daddy Rabbit came driving up and said he'd changed his mind and he and Miss Bessie got married and they took me in on a permanent basis."

"That's an awful lot to happen on short notice," said Roman.

"I didn't mean it would all have to take place at one time. Just so he comes back today." He went on to say he thought it was highly possible that Daddy Rabbit would return. "Today's Saturday," he said, "and he might just be finishing out a week of work." Then he chuckled. "I'd like to see that crowd what's coming to get me when they find out I ain't going with 'em."

Roman smiled. "It would pleasure me to give 'em the news."

"You could answer the door," continued Skinny, "and I'd be peeking around the corner just to see their faces." He tried to make his voice as deep as Roman's and gave the speech that was to be used. "I'm sorry you came out of your way for nothing, folks, but there ain't nobody at this-here hotel going to the orphans' home."

They both laughed. "Maybe Peachy ought to serve the men a glass of lemonade on the front porch," continued Skinny, "so they won't be too put out by the turn of events." Suddenly he became serious. "I got so carried away, I was beginning to believe it," he murmured, walking back toward the hotel.

Nobody came for him during the morning, and in the kitchen after lunch he was saying, "Maybe they ain't coming," when the doorbell rang. "Maybe that's Daddy Rabbit," he said, hurrying to answer it. He put on his white coat as he passed the broom closet.

A tall young man wearing tan slacks and a checkered sport shirt was at the front door. He asked, "Is this the hotel?"

Skinny said, "Yes siree, it sure is," and stepped onto the porch so the caller could see his white coat. "What can I do for you?"

The young man said, "You must be Skinny."

"How'd you know that?" Skinny asked, smiling hospitably.

The man said, "I'm from the orphans' home," and Skinny's smile vanished and he drew back several steps. He stared at the man and then stammered, "I—I thought a whole gang of *old men* were coming." The young man laughed, and Skinny finished by saying, "The preacher ain't even along."

"I stopped by there, but he had been called away," said the visitor, holding out his hand. "I'm Parker Ross and I'm pleased to meet you."

Skinny shook hands, saying, "I'm Skinny."

"And you're not pleased to meet me and I don't blame you."

"Oh, it ain't nothing personal, Mr. Ross."

Parker Ross laughed again. "Call me Parker," he said, "since you've already figured out that I'm not an old man." Then he looked around and added, "This is a nice-looking hotel."

"Would you care to see the rest of it?"

"Sure," said Parker, walking inside. They went upstairs first, and Skinny showed off various rooms. At the end of the hall he reached down and patted R. F. D., who had tagged after them. "This is my dog," he explained. "Me and him used to live on a farm."

"Would you like to bring him to the orphanage?" asked Parker.

"Could I?"

"I'm in charge of the house you'll be living in," Parker said, "and we don't have a pet. The other houses have a dog or a cat, so it'll be all right if you'd like to bring him."

Skinny said happily, "Did you hear that, R. F. D?" and reached down to pat the dog again, but he had disappeared.

Parker stopped to look at a picture on the wall, and Skinny walked across to the head of the staircase. He saw Miss Bessie at the table near the front door, arranging a bowl of dahlias. R. F. D. was there too. He had hopped into a chair and was sitting with his head cocked to one side. Miss Bessie sat down beside him, and they both studied the flowers.

Skinny turned back to Parker Ross. "That room behind you is the biggest bedroom in the hotel," he said, leading the way into it.

Inside he lowered his voice to make certain he would not be overheard. "I've changed my mind about my dog. I don't want to take him with me."

Parker Ross looked puzzled.

"Miss Bessie has already been called on to give up Daddy Rabbit," said Skinny. "He was a friend of hers. And now she's sorry to see me go. I wouldn't feel right to take R. F. D. too."

"I'm sure she will understand," said Parker. "I'll ask her for you."

Skinny looked him straight in the eyes. "I'd appreciate it if you didn't," he said earnestly, and Parker agreed not to mention it.

Downstairs, Miss Bessie was surprised to learn who Parker was. "I thought you were somebody looking for a room," she said.

"I was just showing him the hotel," explained Skinny.

Miss Bessie invited them to come and drink iced tea with her, but they decided it was time to begin the trip. If they set out now they could arrive by suppertime.

Skinny asked, as he and Parker went to get the trunk, "Will I have to go to bed as soon as I eat supper? I've heard tell that's the way it works."

Parker smiled. "Of course not. Let's see, this is Saturday—tonight we'll probably stay up and listen to the 'Barn Dance' on the radio. Then we'll sit on the porch and tell stories. How does that strike you?"

"All right, I guess," said Skinny, not sounding as if it did.

"You won't like it at first," said Parker, reaching over and brushing Skinny's hair back. "I won't try to make you believe that you will. Instead I'll just be honest: it takes a while to get used to it."

Skinny said, "I reckon you've seen others like me get accustomed to it?"

Parker looked at him. "When I was your age I went through it myself." He put the trunk over his broad shoulders and started from the room.

Miss Bessie and Peachy and Roman came outside to wave them off. Skinny patted R. F. D., who chose to stand on the porch instead of coming into the yard with the others. Next he thanked Miss Bessie for all the kind deeds. After that he advised Roman to stay out of stabbing scrapes that might land him back in the chain gang.

Then he came to Peachy, who was dabbing at one eye with the corner of her apron. He said, "You know what I'm gonna do, Peachy? I'm gonna write you a letter."

Peachy smiled, "Why, child, you can't write."

Skinny said cheerily, "I'm gonna learn."

That put everybody in a better frame of mind, and Skinny hopped into the front seat.

Peachy said, "Even if you writes me a letter, I couldn't read it."

"Then I'll come back and read it to you," said Skinny. Pointing ahead as the car started off, he added, "It's only forty miles away."

Word reached Miss Bessie toward the end of September that Skinny was well and that he had settled in nicely to life at the orphanage. Further news was not received until just before Thanksgiving, when the following letter arrived at the hotel:

Dear Miss Bessie and Roman and Peachy,

My friend Dave is writing this letter for me. I have learned to write, but not enough to spell everything yet. Dave is writing because he knows how. He is one of my friends.

I have a lot of friends and they are my age. Most of them are in the seventh grade. Except Joe. He is as far behind as I am but we are learning. Me and Joe.

I hope that you are all fine, and R. F. D., too. One of my jobs is to work in the dairy. They have machines that do the milking. I get to hook the cows up to the machines. I will tell you about it when I come Christmas. I can stay two weeks.

The milking barn is washed every day. Even the floor. Did you ever hear of such a thing? Joe says hello. Dave is going to help him write a letter next to somebody he knows.

Good-by,
Skinny